MISSION
CATASTROPHE

London & Middlesex

Edited By Machaela Gavaghan

First published in Great Britain in 2019 by:

Young Writers
Remus House
Coltsfoot Drive
Peterborough
PE2 9BF
Telephone: 01733 890066
Website: www.youngwriters.co.uk

FOREWORD

Young Writers was created in 1991 with the express purpose of promoting and encouraging creative writing. Each competition we create is tailored to the relevant age group, hopefully giving each student the inspiration and incentive to create their own piece of work, whether it's a poem or a short story. We truly believe that seeing their work in print gives students a sense of achievement and pride in their work and themselves.

Our Survival Sagas series, starting with Mission Catastrophe and followed by Mission Contamination and Mission Chaos, aimed to challenge both the young writers' creativity and their survival skills! One of the biggest challenges, aside from facing floods, avoiding avalanches and enduring epic earthquakes, was to create a story with a beginning, middle and end in just 100 words!

Inspired by the theme of catastrophe, their mission was to craft tales of destruction and redemption, new beginnings and struggles of survival against the odds. As you will discover, these students rose to the challenge magnificently and we can declare *Mission Catastrophe* a success.

The mini sagas in this collection are sure to set your pulses racing and leave you wondering with each turn of the page: are these writers born survivors?

CONTENTS

Clio Ellington (17)	53	Latifa Sheikh Wali (14)	93
Wiktoria Kamila Lajborek (15)	54	Ami Marks (12)	94
Rasha Abbas (13)	55	Zubaida Chowdhury (15)	95
		Saffron Gardner (12)	96

Hornsey School For Girls, London

		Silvia Hajdari (12)	97
		Chloe Turner (12)	98
Fitsum Samuel (13)	56	Lola Meaden (15)	99
Holly O'Connor (15)	57	Rachel Little (14)	100
Isobel Sapphire Dobbie (12)	58		
Fadhail Sharif (11)	59		

Kingsbury High School, Kingsbury

Maryam Ahmed (14)	60		
Naila Elinam Amegashitsi (14)	61	Simran Joshi (12)	101
Thara Amegashitsi (14)	62	Anjali Pradipcumar (13)	102
Syeda Sadia Ali (11)	63	Nicole Shamloo (13)	103
Elisa De Abreu (15)	64	Romaissa Ennasry (12)	104
Samantha Hopkinson (11)	65	Maxim Pudlo (13)	105
Leanne Murphy (15)	66	Hams Youssef (13)	106
Jasmine Dooney (15)	67	Deborah Brobbey (12)	107
Isra Mohamud (12)	68	Sara Sayeed (13)	108
Jennifer Heymann (14)	69	Shahad Sharif (13)	109
Foos Abdulahi (14)	70	Mujtaba Ahmad (13)	110
Kadija Mohamed (15)	71	David Cyrus Bahrami (12)	111
Keeley Daniella	72	Sara Tillaih (13)	112
O'Callaghan (12)		Sara Alexia Iordan (12)	113
Maryan Bashir Farah (13)	73	Vinusan Padmarasa (12)	114
Magdalena Peric (14)	74	Kody Nembhard Dale (12)	115
Verdi Mbumba (13)	75	Avni Kiran Hirani (12)	116
Roqia Matin (14)	76	Vanajan Subaskaran (13)	117
Saadath Ali (15)	77	Nour Jaafar (13)	118
Ohemaa Blankson (15)	78	Suxin He (13)	119
Atosa Juliet Mohammadian (13)	79	Zaid Tahir (12)	120
Millie Hoare (11)	80	Ayanna Grant-Wright (13)	121
Samina Ahmed (15)	81	Dhea Kerai (12)	122
Irem Kademlioglu (15)	82	Akshay Pradipcumar (13)	123
Noora Younes (13)	83	Kiran Sivakumar (13)	124
Emily Marks (14)	84	Anoj Roy (12)	125
Khadidja Cheref (13)	85	Sora Sherif (13)	126
Jannat Ahmed (14)	86	Diya Khetani (13)	127
Syeda Nazifa Khatun (14)	87	Abderrahime Hamadache (13)	128
Venus Sanjeewa (2)	88	Theodor Purav (12)	129
Mischa Serugo (12)	89	Nazifa Ahmed (13)	130
Isobel Carter (11)	90	Hussainali Sachoo (12)	131
Iva Shehu (13)	91	Nyal Hirani (13)	132
Sheyda Shamshin Lalehiloo (13)	92	Courtney Martindale (13)	133

THE MINI SAGAS

The Unlucky Disaster

There was once a group of scientists and a man called Josh. He was a young, intelligent and curious person.

One day, they went to see how animals lived in outer space. All of a sudden, after flying for two weeks, they crash-landed on an undiscovered planet. The crash was terrible. Josh found a huge volcano bigger than the one on Mars. The crash resulted in a devastating earthquake. They were all scared, terrified. The earthquake was so bad, it shifted boulders and resulted in the volcano erupting. "Argh, run!"

Mohammed Adam Mirza (12)
Ark Academy, Wembley

The Big Burn

Porphyria? Never heard of it. Yet here I am in an inky-black room. It's midsummer and every beam of light is unbearable. As the gaunt curtains slide, a small passageway of light enters the room, the reddish hue of light is beautiful. I don't realise the ray is carving a charcoal print into the wall. The curtains shift, the light now falling onto my cheekbone. I can feel my skin peeling. I am unrecognisable. My last breath escapes my lips. I understand that, on my lonely journey to the beyond, I will soon be accompanied. The heatwave has begun...

Amima Hayat (11)
Ayesha Siddiqa Girls' School, Southall

School Is The Death Of Me!

It was a typical Monday, I was ready to get home. I headed into my form room to be dismissed but was interrupted by a horrible scream. Then, I noticed the windows, there was water right up to the window. *Impossible,* I thought. We were on the third floor! Quickly, I snapped back to reality and turned my head left and right to look for a solution. "Aha! Let's use the tables as rafts and metre sticks to push!" I suggested.

I headed to the first table... of bullies! Just before reaching safety, *splash!* I was drowning...

Mahbuba Rahman (12)
Ayesha Siddiqa Girls' School, Southall

Unexpected

As I tried to drink my tea, the floor kept shaking, allowing my tea to escape from its boiling cup, warming me up with its embracement.
After two minutes, I'd had enough! I stomped angrily towards the front door but something from the window caught my attention. I had seen many things, like people like me being taken for slavery, but nothing like this! A massive chunk of the building next to mine was falling in midair. Underneath, there was a mum and her two sons, ready to be squashed by the square monster above them. There was an earthquake!

Sarah Wahbi Mohammed (11)
Ayesha Siddiqa Girls' School, Southall

Scorching Rocks

I mopped the sweat off my face as smoke came bubbling out of the pot-like volcano. I stumbled down the rough, burnt rocks as my feet sent messages to my body, pleading for help. Suddenly, a rock came flying down, resting on my leg. My eyes widened in fear. "I-I'm going to burn to death!" I charged at the scorching rock with all my hand's strength. Tears trickled down my eyes like two waterfalls racing each other. Then, I heard the wailing of a helicopter and hope filled the air, but they didn't come in time.

Sheza Chaudry (11)
Ayesha Siddiqa Girls' School, Southall

Coming Closer

The whole world was in danger. The sun had come closer and already, Mars and Mercury had been destroyed. We were next. Just yesterday, my uncle had called to tell me that his house had melted. There was no water to drink, all the world's water had dried up like a desert. Many people who were afraid of death dug deep tunnels underground to stop themselves from burning. Animals were dying, people were dying, my whole family died, except for me and my mother, in front of me. I watched their bodies slowly turn white...

Ilhaan Wehliye (11)
Ayesha Siddiqa Girls' School, Southall

Death By Heat

The smell of burnt rubber was whisked up into the air. People ran for shade under trees, but the leaves succumbed to the heat. Water was a blessing if found. I wiped the sweat off my face to find my T-shirt drenched. *Water,* I thought. I looked up to see the clear sky. The sun tortured us with its powerful rays. I could feel my body roasting. How would I survive? I wasn't going to die like this. I would live. I had to! Maybe I could move to Antarctica, but that would be a bit of a long-shot...

Aisha Omar (11)
Ayesha Siddiqa Girls' School, Southall

Stranded On An Island

I heard birds screeching, trees rustling, the wind howling and the waves colliding off the rocks. I suddenly felt pain crawling down my legs. I smelt salt and fish, but mostly danger.

I opened my eyes, hoping to wake up in my luxurious bed but instead, I saw a blinding light. I saw green, tropical trees, a sapphire sun, yellow sand beneath my body and the foamy, blue waves. I got up to see litres of blood gushing out of the wounds on my legs. How did I even end up here? What was I going to do?

Sabah Hussain (11)
Ayesha Siddiqa Girls' School, Southall

The Verge Of Death

The unbearable cold weather sent a chill down my spine. I climbed up the colossal, snowy, white mountain and I dug a massive hole in it. I reached the peak at last! All of a sudden, with a smash, there was an avalanche. I felt it was almost the end of my life. I jumped off the shrinking mountain as it crumbled to dust.

As I jumped off the mountain with my parachute, there was another avalanche as I was about to land. I was at the end of my life...

Maryama Bashir (11)
Ayesha Siddiqa Girls' School, Southall

The Desolation

Gradually, I peeled open my eyes to witness the atrocious destruction - everything swallowed by the ground! Everything gone. My eyes froze like an icy puddle, robbing me of warmth. I could smell the impenetrable smoke hanging in the air, shifting like a ghost in the breeze, preying on the ruins. The perpetual cacophony of crows obscured the skeletons of the houses. Despair was like concrete in my veins. A sudden thought electrocuted me, reminding me of my family. The memory of my family pummelled my soul, reminding me of my loved ones' agony. Everything was swallowed by the ground...

Maliha Khan (15)
Copthall School, Mill Hill

The Nightmare Of Your Reality

Red, blood-red specifically. It engulfed me, it seeped into my skin, right towards my spine. It lured me, I shouldn't have followed but it was too luscious to ignore. The hunger in me grew, the urge too strong that just the smell of the crimson blood accelerated my control into a void. Was it careless? Probably, but I didn't care! I didn't care that I'd deprived humanity to the brim of existence. I didn't care about the bodies surrounding me. I was a beast, the reason why I enjoyed the thrill and why I relished in the sound of agony...

Yllka Azemi (12)
Greenford High School, Southall

History's Voice

Debris, mankind's legacy unravels as nothing more than debris. It floats by as delicate as the frail attachment of a dandelion. Footprints of broken families and misguided religions merge with its final chapter branded with unified carnage and sweet neglect, whispers of the wind confess their failures. Lost souls hiss, the shattered winds dance to our graves under the empty nuclear cage. Here lies our broken world. May those who inherit it learn from our mistakes and banish the fatal stakes to guard the choice of 'history's voice'.

Gayatri Pandya (17)
Greenford High School, Southall

Swim Or Drown!

The water fills my lungs but I manage to swim. Suddenly, the air surrounding me changes into harsh shards of icicles created from water vapour. This is it, isn't it? Life will disappear. No, it can't end like this! An area covered by mist can slowly be seen. People are crying, begging for mercy to the gods. It's too late. We will only be able to survive from one choice - swim or drown. But on the other side, I can see people pushing kids into the water, only worried about themselves! Is this the end?

Aneeqa Khan (13)
Greenford High School, Southall

Russian Revenge

Boom! Another chopper exploded violently in the air while the military jets tore through the skies, chasing the stolen choppers. "This is Peter Richards from the British Secret Service. Code red! I repeat, code red! Reporting from Moscow!"
Back in London, things were getting way more serious, the offices at 10 Downing Street and other government buildings were packed. Nobody knew what was going on.
Back at MI5's headquarters, a transmission came in from Moscow. This one was not verified. Suddenly, all the power in the nation turned off, it was a catastrophe! There was a massive cyber attack...

Jagveer Singh Sunner (14)
Guru Nanak Sikh Academy, Hayes

In Which He Saves A Soul, For Himself At Least

"Any last words, O'Brian?" his voice cackled as he sliced through his victim's already bruised chest. A scream erupted, making him smirk. Suddenly, a little, high-pitched voice cried out in front of him. It was a little human, too short for its own good. Guessing the victim was her father, his smile grew wider. But something in him ignited, he saw those little, saddened twinkles in her eyes. He took two long strides before crouching down before her. His claws wiped over her tears as she stood afraid and shocked.

"Are you going to kill me?" she asked. He smirked...

Chajieena Chandran (14)
Guru Nanak Sikh Academy, Hayes

World's End...

"Everything is shaking!" You knew the time was going to come one day, and the time had finally arrived. "Guys, head out, now!" you screamed as you ran out of your house, taking your little brother along with you. You looked around and saw madness, catastrophe and insanity. You ran. You didn't know where you were going. You noticed everyone was running the other way. Suddenly, a large crack appeared between your legs! You nearly fell into the darkness of the earth. You were stuck so you let go of your brother. "I'm sorry, I love you!" *Whoosh!*

Sneha Das Moyna (13)
Guru Nanak Sikh Academy, Hayes

War Life

"Come on! Attack from the side!" I could see dead corpses with their souls giving me courage. My fellow people were dying in front of me. I could hear a fearless soldier keeping our morale up. We *had* to win. "Use the air force!" We were surrounded by enemies. Courageously, I stepped into the middle of the battlefield, shooting as many soldiers as I could. I got shot four times and remembered every memory with my family, my graduation, getting many professional awards and the only dream I had was to serve my country. Finally, I dropped and approached Heaven.

Bavneet Singh (13)

Guru Nanak Sikh Academy, Hayes

The Terrible Disaster

Bang! Another explosion took place, killing many innocent people. Saffron was disgusted by the people that led out these horrible and menacing attacks. She was against them and wanted to end all of this. She said to herself, "It's time to take action!" She decided too that she wanted those dreadful, horrendous, awful people to be punished for their deeds. Saffron couldn't see those guiltless people dying in front of her eyes. Suddenly, she saw a person put something down. She crept closer. It was a treacherous bomb! "Oh no!" Silence occurred...

Saffron Kaur Bains (14)
Guru Nanak Sikh Academy, Hayes

World War X

Screaming, shouting, blood. This covered the atmosphere of America. The virus spread through the streets, filling America with demonic people. Michael ran quickly to safety with his fellow soldiers. Everyone, whoever could fit, bombarded the planes and boats. America was a danger zone with a war between zombies and humans. Michael was assigned to a mission with soldiers and a doctor. Limited supplies and weapons led them to a lab research centre. They were surrounded by zombies and drugs. The soldiers battled bravely. Michael took the lead, the cure was there...

Keshav Kumar (13)
Guru Nanak Sikh Academy, Hayes

The Empire Strikes

Buildings being destroyed, tree after tree tumbling onto the ground, Moses is driving down Springfield Road, trying to find people to help, but everybody he drives by is dead or seconds away from dying. Suddenly, he sees a spaceship crashing down and hitting the school's car park. Moses goes down to investigate. It is dark, he can't see a lot. Then he sees bodies coming towards him. It's the aliens! Not knowing what to do, he takes out his sword and slashes them into pieces. Unexpectedly, he is cornered as an army of aliens come towards him...

Jasraj Sran (13)
Guru Nanak Sikh Academy, Hayes

Argh! Christmas Is Destroyed!

Zoe watched the Christmas tree flickering, excited as a snowman with clothes, she was ready for the suspense of this special day. She looked down and screamed, "Where are the presents?" She looked everywhere from head to toe but she couldn't find them. She heard a noise. She picked up the star from the top of the Christmas tree. She tiptoed through the hallway. There it was, the thief! She rushed slowly to the culprit, trying not to make a sound. She was right behind it. She got her star ready and secure but when she turned... *boom!*

Tejinder Chana (13)
Guru Nanak Sikh Academy, Hayes

Zake's Unfortunate Events

It was a rainy day. Lightning was striking. We were on our way to our grandma's house. My dad was struggling while driving because he'd forgotten his glasses. My mum was hesitant of driving because of the weather. While we were on the way, the fuel sign flashed.

The petrol station was two hours away. We had to try and make it.

Halfway through, the car started to splutter so we stopped at the hard shoulder. In a split second, we were ambushed by three men. They had knives. They slaughtered my family. I called the police and hoped...

Jaskirat Singh Chohan (13)
Guru Nanak Sikh Academy, Hayes

World War Internet

A catastrophe drove everyone wild. They were hungry, hungry for the Internet! Yes, our generation was the most 'connected' than any other, but there was a group of people who wanted that to stop. They wanted the ancient ways back, when humans lived in mud huts and grew food and hunted animals with spears instead of technology. They hated the name of it. I believed that the progress of humanity was meant to happen, but the organisation (LIV) exploited the people and turned this once beautiful world into a disaster. No one could stop them...

Tirath Virk (13)
Guru Nanak Sikh Academy, Hayes

Grief, Blood And Death - Dystopia

Blood streaming around the bodies of the innocent, the instant havoc around a once ambient atmosphere fills my hazy vision with salty tears. I hear the fading yearnings of vulnerable children all around in this apocalyptic scene. What has this world become? Shrapnel scattered on the floor, fire fumes float in the air. The revelation of the kryptonic army has destroyed many lives during this unfortunate event. Anyone who is still left on our motherland will too be wiped out one day. I'm Sophie Parker and this is my end, will it be yours too?

Harsheen Momi (13)
Guru Nanak Sikh Academy, Hayes

Hiroshima

Andrew Nelson, a courageous hero from Hiroshima, Japan, has not forgotten about the depressing bombing the cold-hearted Americans hosted. Andrew is heartbroken and wants to get revenge.

One evening in 1995, Mr Nelson mysteriously buys a rocket launcher and an assault rifle and then travels to America. All of a sudden, he sees the president staring and pointing at him from a humongous building. Quietly and patiently, Andrew gets in the elevator, then he sees Barack Obama. This provokes Andrew's reaction to being severely furious...

Jaskaran Lall (13)
Guru Nanak Sikh Academy, Hayes

The Only One

It was our last meal together. It wasn't until we heard the deafening screams that we knew about their arrival. They came in mass numbers with these weird, monstrous-looking spaceships. I did what I could to protect the little ones. The buildings began to erode. I took my family to the nearest train station. I heard the shrieks and cries of women and their babies. I tried to fight off as many as I could using an old, wooden, kitchen knife. It wasn't until I looked around that I was able to see that I was the only one remaining...

Simran Aujla (14)
Guru Nanak Sikh Academy, Hayes

The End

At one o'clock in the morning, an alarm went, stating that the world would end at 2pm. Harry instantly sprinted out of his room and turned on the TV to watch the news. Harry burst out crying. He didn't know what to do. He didn't know who to call, who to see, what to do. He instantly called his mum and said goodbye. Unfortunately, she lived on the other side of the world so he couldn't see her.

Ten hours later, it was 12pm.

An hour later, it was 1:59pm. There were fifty seconds left... then *bang!*

Ansh Kamboj (13)
Guru Nanak Sikh Academy, Hayes

Doomsday

Breathless, broken, lightheaded, I know if I don't run into this abandoned house, it will be the end, the end of humanity. I can feel the intense heat on the back of my neck. As I open the door, I firmly take hold of my necklace saying, "I love you, Mum." Whilst holding my necklace, I notice my skin has started to burn.

Minutes later, I collapse on the ground. The flames grow larger and as they try to touch my necklace, there is a loud bang.

Seconds later, a place that I once called home is now destroyed.

Gurkirat Plahe (13)

Guru Nanak Sikh Academy, Hayes

The Threatening Tsunami

The floor shook beneath her wheelchair. It trembled and quaked, getting louder every second. Everywhere Saskia looked, all she saw was fog. Being alone on the beach ruined her chances of getting home. Darkness spread around her and covered the sea. The sea was coming towards her like an animal after its prey. Was she the prey? Every shout for help was drowned out by the sound of the tsunami. It was coming closer. She got as far away as she could from it but there was no one to help, it was just her and the threatening tsunami...

Sharleen Kaur Lakhanpal (13)

Guru Nanak Sikh Academy, Hayes

Destruction

Day and night, one after another, innocent people see the end, expecting it as we all hide behind the demolished, destroyed buildings. Blood, bodies, rainclouds, the bodies lay everywhere, reminding our souls that the unknown organisations will make sure not one person survives. The fires, the protests will not stop. My name is Kaia and I am prepared to do whatever it takes to get everything back. Sitting here in the corner, my heart pounding as loud as thunder, I recall my parents disappearing, they both started this...

Jessika Kapur (13)
Guru Nanak Sikh Academy, Hayes

Audaciously

Here I was, sitting on my congenial sofa. As I stared through my passage, a sudden noise reverberated. I thought that I was just imagining things but I wasn't, it hit again. I sprang off the sofa and scampered to the window in fear. As I glared through the window, something extensive was in front of me. I only had a couple of minutes to escape. Overwhelming panic became a stone in my chest. I scampered to my door in fear as bits of my house started to get swallowed up in the tornado. Audaciously, I gave up my life.

Deep Singh Sahota (13)
Guru Nanak Sikh Academy, Hayes

A Bad Feeling

Ben was lying in his bed, unable to sleep, listening to the wind howling and the rain lashing hard against his bedroom window. The weather was often like this in October but from past experiences, he knew that the river would get very high and close to bursting its banks. He got up to check and opened the living room window at the front of his house to peer out into the darkness. Ben was afraid that a flood would come tomorrow. He told his mum that he wanted to go to another country, his mum didn't want to go...

Kiruthika Pirabalan (11)
Guru Nanak Sikh Academy, Hayes

Meteor Devastation

The peaceful world is coming to an end as the mouth of death is gradually opening, ready to swallow the innocent people. My friends and I are trying to meticulously run away from the meteors, which are continuously following us. Everywhere we go, there are meteors lying on the ground. No one knows what's caused this, they are swallowing all the humans. We all try to be as tentative as possible but the shadow of meteors are blinding us. As my droopy eyes slowly close, struggling to catch my breath, I collapse...

Ajmit Kaur (13)
Guru Nanak Sikh Academy, Hayes

The Evil AI

Yes, finally, it was finished. He had finally made artificial intelligence, it was beautiful! Time to activate it. "Hello, I am an AI. How may I assist you?"
Dr Smith was proud of himself. He went home to rest, but what he didn't know was that the AIs in the lab wanted to take over the world. Dr Smith went back to work. The AIs threatened him. Luckily, he escaped. He tried to shut them down, but they started to pretend to be him! The people tried to help Dr Smith, but what were they going to do?

Taranveer Hira (13)
Guru Nanak Sikh Academy, Hayes

Hitler Comes Back...

It was an ordinary day in Germany but then, it happened. Adolf Hitler came back to life! He was still an evil, cruel and short-tempered man. He wanted to eliminate the whole world but not his supporters or his kind. He wanted to become a leader again and, if that didn't happen, people would die. He had many resources to make sure he got his way. These included guns and tanks. He had already killed ten people and would kill more if he wasn't made leader soon. Would you make him the leader or suffer death?

Jia Kaur Bhachu (14)
Guru Nanak Sikh Academy, Hayes

The Constant Barrage Of Bombs

How did any of them survive? There were bombs and then, zilch. I wasn't too close to the explosion, which is what kept me safe. All these people were in the blast radius. I wanted to ask what happened, if we were safe. I heard the screams of people calling to missing people that didn't survive. I ran into a house, if you could call it that. The television was on displaying an urgent message. 'Bombs are falling on London!' I sprinted outside and was greeted by loud bangs, there was nothing left...

Maninder Singh Saggu (13)
Guru Nanak Sikh Academy, Hayes

The Wild Woods

All four friends sang their way along the mysterious path. They were all excited for the road trip, especially Thomas, he was always looking for a reason to party! Suddenly, the car started making noises and came to a halt. They got out and saw that they were stranded in the middle of some isolated woods. This was a disaster! Then, they heard a threatening noise, it sounded like a bear. Lucas and Billy jumped up. Thomas picked up a stick for protection. What were they going to do in these terrifying, wild woods?

Manveen Kaur (12)
Guru Nanak Sikh Academy, Hayes

Blood, Tears And Horror!

Tears of blood were rolling down her cheeks as she saw her only sister die in front of her eyes. Jacy was now an only child. Her sister was not the only one who died. Almost ninety percent of the world had died! Jacy's sister, Anna, had been murdered by Scott! He was going to each country and killing as many people as he could. The remaining ten percent said he was dead because he hadn't killed anyone for weeks. However, Jacy kept seeing someone following her.
The next day, she had been killed too!

Ravneet Kaur (14)
Guru Nanak Sikh Academy, Hayes

Nuclear Accident

"Incoming!" someone shouted. Uday, Josh and Donald took cover under Josh's shield. They were disgusted and amazed at the amount of damage dealt to Josh's shield of justice. Donald damaged the nuclear bomb mid-air with a kick. They all looked up and ran, awaiting the next attack from the Germans. Uday sliced two bombs in a row, which caused the bomb to be diffused. Donald, Josh and Uday were hurt, they were losing blood. Donald saw another bomb coming towards them, he ran towards the bomb...

Udayveer Ghatoura (14)
Guru Nanak Sikh Academy, Hayes

The Crashing Plane

Everything seemed to be perfect before we boarded that plane that snatched all of our happiness away in one go. It was the first good trip I was going on, but it turned out to be the last. The plane's front wheels were not coming out and the pilot was frightened. We only had one option, which was to get our parachutes and jump out of the plane, but the doors were also locked. We were helpless, frightened, scared and terrified. The only thing in our minds was death. We had no chance of escaping...

Jasraj Singh (13)
Guru Nanak Sikh Academy, Hayes

Zombies! Die!

Five teenagers survive the outrageous catastrophe. Blood oozes from millions of bodies on the gross ground. Families are all dead. Zombies surround the city of New York. Jack, Ben, Sophie, Katrina and Tom are the only survivors from the apocalypse. Guns and swords are in their hands, ready to fight. The zombies are slow, weak and easy to kill. The five teenagers try to save the planet and rebuild everything to make it safe again but the zombies start fighting again, and the fight still continues...

Karsan Kirupananthaparathyar (13)
Guru Nanak Sikh Academy, Hayes

The Catastrophic Never-Ending Cave

I was running as if there was no tomorrow. My cheeks flooded with tears, all I had was a map, which made no sense. I felt something grasp my ankle. It felt disgusting, it was slimy with rough... hands, more like branches. I had no courage to turn around to see it, it was already too much... It all started when I was dared by those girls to go near the woods. My weakness struck and I walked in with curiosity. Wandering too much, I regretted it now I was stuck in this never-ending cave...

Nametha Navaneethan (13)
Guru Nanak Sikh Academy, Hayes

Corrupt

It was a rainy day, everything seemed normal. I reached my home, walked in and I was attacked! I assumed someone was ruthlessly robbing my home. They decided to ruthlessly stab me five times until my screams were worthless. What was I now? I was there, just not alive, yet I could still control my body like it was a machine. My body, emotionless on the ground, fully red, I started to get up. Those monstrosities of beings were leaving. I took the knife I was stabbed with and killed them...

Revin Manivannan (13)
Guru Nanak Sikh Academy, Hayes

Rocking Dead

I heard the zombies roaring, I heard the women screaming, I heard the men shouting, I heard the babies crying, I heard the vehicles crashing.
I was now all alone, the dead walking right in front of the window. All I could do was either sit in silence or go out and become one of those horrible, ugly, bloody creatures with body parts hanging out like chandeliers from the roof. Crying, I left the apartment. Walking past the red blood, I took all my weapons to the walking dead...

Vinny Singh Bajaj (13)
Guru Nanak Sikh Academy, Hayes

The Cries

A shrill cry echoed in the mist, it had to have been a mile away. Shannon had recently heard a lot of these sounds over the past week. She was intrigued.

After about an hour, she heard another scream. She ran to the front door and picked up the pre-packed bag. She followed the piercing scream until she suddenly tripped and grazed her forehead. Ignoring the blood, she got up, realising she had fallen next to a crack. She looked around, there were knee-deep cracks everywhere...

Gursharan Dhillon (13)
Guru Nanak Sikh Academy, Hayes

Fighting For A World Without Resources

The year is 2040. It's been exactly one week since they came. A flash of light has beamed through the sky, an alien spaceship as big as the city of New York has shot a flare of light at Earth without warning and it has disintegrated all manmade buildings and materials and collected them, all of this was in the blink of an eye. My name is Lewis and I'm a survivor. I have moved to Kenya from England. England is a death trap. Now I face a world of savages and barbarians...

Satpal Chaha (14)
Guru Nanak Sikh Academy, Hayes

During The Worst Time

I could hear gunshots and bombs. I was shocked, I thought I was going to die. I knew I needed to escape that second to prevent myself from dying. I was sad and depressed. I hadn't seen my family for twelve months, I really missed my mum and dad and my baby brother, who was now a grown-up. It started pouring with rain. I was soaked. I wasn't going to run across the field, I was very scared. I didn't know what the future would bring. Hopefully, I would survive...

Daya Sangha (14)
Guru Nanak Sikh Academy, Hayes

Jack And His Unforgettable Time

I am Jack and I live in the forest. It is a dark and cramped but peaceful place. I enjoy it here. I live on the trees and use leaves for clothes. I hear the wind blowing loudly. It is loud and scary. The trees sway really fast, some of them rub their branches together. The sounds get louder. It's the first time it's happened. I don't know what's happening. Suddenly, the trees are on fire. Where will I go? I remember I have ropes to save myself!

Bineeta Kaur Taneja (13)
Guru Nanak Sikh Academy, Hayes

Small Pox - The Story

It was 8:30 in the morning when Tatlin woke up and found out a horrific truth, something that would change her whole future. Everyone she knew had smallpox and she needed to do something about it and fast. This could ruin a lot of lives within a very small amount of time. She knew that there would be a cure because, if there wasn't, an apocalypse would take place and she couldn't let that happen. She would do anything it took to find the cure...

Jazleen Singh (14)
Guru Nanak Sikh Academy, Hayes

The Bomb That Ruined Lives

I didn't know what had happened. I wanted answers but I didn't get any. I still remember...
I was walking to my local church with my parents. As soon as we reached it, my life changed. My parents' and siblings' lives ended. It was now only me. That one bomb ruined my entire life. Now look where I am, stuck in a weird refugee camp. From a lovely family, to this. From lovely knitted clothes to sacks. Why God? Why would you do this?

Diya Kaur (14)
Guru Nanak Sikh Academy, Hayes

The Blazing Fire

Tom was in his house all alone when there was a blazing fire and he couldn't do anything! He tried to leave the house but the door was locked and the keys were on fire. He couldn't call anyone because his phone was on fire. The thing that caused the fire was his Xbox, it had blown up. His family were out and his neighbours were asleep. He couldn't do anything...

Randeep Sidhu (14)
Guru Nanak Sikh Academy, Hayes

Panic At Pacific

The raging sea awakens from its deep slumber, throwing itself aggressively through the dark, stormy night, electrifying lightning strikes through the sky. Terror-stricken Harry fights for his dear life in the deep waters of the Pacific Ocean. Loud growls and angry screeches force the blue currents towards the ship. The battle between Harry and the monstrous hurricane at sea continues. Difficulty navigating, Harry loses control, unaware of the frozen icebergs ahead of him. Panicking with fear and confusion, trying to locate a route to escape, the sea is ready to swallow and take the lives of the hundreds on board...

Jaini Anand (11)
Hatch End High School, Hatch End

The End Or A New Beginning?

It was Thursday 17th of May, 2017, a time of ill-ruin in America. A disease called Nigelose consisted of a bacteria that you could not see with the naked eye, only with distinct scientific goggles. However, this only affected adults from forty years old and up. The president of the United States of America thought enough was enough. Madam President instructed a special scientist to create a vaccination serum to protect the next generation. As I was gathering all my equipment, unexpectedly, the lab doors slammed shut with a metallic chime. A voice alarmed, "Ten minutes until permanent lockdown!"

Clio Ellington (17)
Hatch End High School, Hatch End

The Last Picture

"Subject #1986, starting log."
"Permission granted." This was it, the last subjects testing the mind control serum. Lara and Brandon were the last ones to volunteer, and it might have been the worst mistake of their entire lives. Brandon knew what was coming next, sharp pain spread through his stomach and infiltrated his whole body. Trembling, his mind was now under their command, but what frightened them the most was that he and Lara had *no* control. His mind could now be trained. The last thing they remembered was the destruction of humanity.

Wiktoria Kamila Lajborek (15)
Hatch End High School, Hatch End

The Locket World

I was playing in my backyard as usual when, suddenly, I heard a crash from where my ball had hit the ground. I decided to explore. I discovered that it was a rusty, old locket. I took interest in it and took it with me. I opened it in my bedroom, a blinding source of light absorbed me into a journey like a pack of wolves hunting for prey. It was another world, where the sky was splitting apart into a blood-red, demonic scar...
I awoke with tumult. It was a dream, or was it?

Rasha Abbas (13)
Hatch End High School, Hatch End

I Can't Help It

It all began in the hospital.

"Everything is normal," the doctor was saying to my parents. "Just lie back and relax."

But I couldn't, I told him quickly. I could smell the flow of blood coming nearer and nearer to the town.

"Is he alright, Doctor?" Mum asked anxiously.

Bang, bang! I ran up to the roof. I could see it all - the tornado had struck! I could see it all - the bloodshed of the innocent people. It was all in my hands, but what could I do? It was the beginning of the catastrophe...

Fitsum Samuel (13)

Hornsey School For Girls, London

The Market

The golden sun beamed down on my face as I strolled to the market for the ingredients for that night's goat curry. In front of me, a large hubbub of locals looked concerned and confused.
"We're not ready! Why did we not know?" were just a couple of distressed phrases that exploded out of their mouths.
I walked cautiously as a dark shadow covered me like a blanket. It was suddenly cold. A deafening rumble of thunder rattled down my spine. The screams of the locals pierced my ears as everyone hurtled away. We were too late. It had arrived...

Holly O'Connor (15)
Hornsey School For Girls, London

Three Days To Animal

There's a theory in ethics: three days to animal. Humans have three days without a vital resource before they turn into animals. I think I've broken the record. One day in the woods, searching for warmth, and I'm already a monster!
"Need warmth," I chatter, shaking.
I scrabble in the snow for a place to stay the night. My cold hands latch onto a rectangular box, a matchbox. With shaking fingers, I light a match but I drop it onto the hard ground. All I can do is watch as the wood and everything in it goes up in flames...

Isobel Sapphire Dobbie (12)
Hornsey School For Girls, London

The Furious Avalanche Strikes Again

It is Sunday, Sarah's favourite day. It's time for ice skating around the snowy mountain. Sarah, who loves being sporty and selfish, leaves her sister in bed and leaves the house, unnoticed, by herself. After reaching the frosty bench, she takes off her shoes and puts on her ice skating shoes. She starts skating and enjoying herself. Suddenly, she sees an avalanche. Rapidly, she looks for her phone and realises she's forgotten it.

Seconds pass and the avalanche comes very close. Sarah tries skating away but twists her leg and can't move! She is too late and never comes back.

Fadhail Sharif (11)
Hornsey School For Girls, London

Hectic Heatwave

Beside me was a town bustling with trepidation. Spiralling steam encompassed the slender birch trees. Without warning, the fire lit the latent grass. Who would have thought that this could happen in Saint Petersburg, Russia? Surrounding me were locals foraging for food. Who was going to survive? My morbid curiosity made me stare at the rocks which were smouldering... in the winter? My diligent eyes bawled at the odious whip of the atrocious fire. Yet the fire was luminous, like pinpoints of light through a prism. Perspiring trees choked in the smog. Solitude became a forlorn friend as death arose...

Maryam Ahmed (14)
Hornsey School For Girls, London

Noah's Ark All Over Again

History has a nasty habit of repeating itself so they should've seen it coming. It's Noah's Ark all over again, but this time, it's not just endless rain: it's raging wildfires and violent earthquakes. Its ceaseless blizzards and volcanic eruptions worse than Mount Vesuvius at Pompeii. A strident cacophony of screams pummel my ears - their cries of anguish and pain are deafening. If I didn't despise these humans so much, I might pity them. But I don't; how can I? They think of themselves more than they think of me. Me! Their Lord. Their creator.

They deserve it all.

Naila Elinam Amegashitsi (14)
Hornsey School For Girls, London

The Day The Water Went Backwards

It had been another predictably hot day in Beia and Ambrosia was alone. Her mother, Professor Maynard-Kelly, had been busy since they'd arrived. Ambrosia only knew one thing - an earthquake might hit Beia. Ambrosia squinted at the sun. Suddenly, the water began retreating backwards. It was as though the ocean was taking a deep breath and sucking in everything at once. What was happening? Hadn't her mother said there was going to be an earthquake? Yes, Ambrosia realised with horror, there was an earthquake; an underwater one. Which meant...
"Tsunami!"

Thara Amegashitsi (14)
Hornsey School For Girls, London

The Furious Flood

A major destructive, persistent even had occurred. The thunder crashed, roar upon roar. The eddying lightning flashed fire in my face and the whirlwinds were whirling dust round and round, spewing remnants into the void from its wake. It was particularly malicious. Odd and indefinable. A bustling scene. A living nightmare, the sound of people crying was everywhere. It was spinning like a bouncy ball being bounced. Buildings tumbling down, no longer existing, so they were demolished and worthless. The loud roar destroying men and threatening many more showing no restraint. The earth lay bare...

Syeda Sadia Ali (11)
Hornsey School For Girls, London

It Comes Home

It came at night. The sable sky suddenly flared carmine and the world's final cataclysm had arrived. Thrashing towards my window, I saw it - the smouldering structure beyond, the size of the most behemoth mountain known to man. The Earth began sinking beneath the ruinous giant's feet as my mother grasped my clammy hand and hauled me out of the house. Chunks of the asteroid plummeted around us, colliding with the crumbling ground. Despite my mother's panicked shrieks and wailing sirens, I dared to glance back. Centuries had passed and it had finally returned home... to destroy us.

Elisa De Abreu (15)
Hornsey School For Girls, London

Deathly Silent

Suddenly, I woke up. I didn't know why, but it was deathly silent. Even the birds were silent. All of a sudden, the ground shook violently. I remembered that my teacher had said, "If the ground shakes, it's an earthquake."
So I got out of bed and ran to safety under my desk. Then a piece of the ceiling landed on the desk, crushing the middle. I froze. I heard my mum screaming my name, "Lizzy, Lizzy, are you okay?"
I got up from under my desk and tried to run to the door, but I couldn't see a thing...

Samantha Hopkinson (11)
Hornsey School For Girls, London

As Eruption Falls

The ground shook vigorously, grumbling vehemently as it began to crumble. Her heart racing frantically, she gathered all of her precious belongings, throwing them hastily inside her suitcase. Looking out of her window, she saw the quivering mountain of eruption, struggling to hold back the urge to explode. Suddenly, fiery vermillion liquid poured down the huge hill! The screams of panicked people ran through the air. Rushing to her car, she attempted to escape the nightmare. However, a huge piece of smoking rock struck her car, sending her crashing down a steep hill, her car in flames...

Leanne Murphy (15)
Hornsey School For Girls, London

Deluge

I remember dreamily gazing at the sapphire-blue ripples of the sea and the twinkling shards of light reflecting off the never-ending blanket of water. There was a sense of perfect tranquility in the air. Little did I know that a few hours later, that same sea would transform into a huge horrific monster... My heart leapt into my mouth as I sprinted away from the towering wave chasing me. I could hear blood-curdling screams all around me. The sound of the wave coming closer made my mind go numb. At that moment, I thought, *this is the end...*

Jasmine Dooney (15)
Hornsey School For Girls, London

Day Of Horror

It was a dark gloomy day. Thick, black, grey clouds started to surround the entire village. But little did everyone know that that day would be a day of destruction and fear. Out of curiosity, a young girl called Ella, who was about twelve, was exploring and trying to find out what was causing the horrible and misfortunate weather.

Finally, after what seemed like years, she saw the most bone-chilling volcano rumbling with anger! It gave her shivers down her spine. Ella started to panic with fear and agony. She knew she had to protect her village...

Isra Mohamud (12)
Hornsey School For Girls, London

The Aftermath

Horrific, scarring, traumatising. That was one way to describe the catastrophe. Yet no words or phrases formed could ever allow a person to fathom the strange event that occurred. Not even a survivor like me could comprehend the unexpected appearance of the unearthly creatures roaming around, destroying the peace and dignity of Earth. They trapped us as though we were their pets and caused us pain, suffering and despair. They watched us slowly diminish. The way they crushed and trampled upon our Earth - abhorrent. But no more dwelling on past events. It was time for revenge...

Jennifer Heymann (14)
Hornsey School For Girls, London

A Battle With The Waves

Waves quickly retreated from the shore, leaving behind soft golden sand which squelched under our feet. The gentle humming of the waves soothed us as the water continued to creep further away. The blinding light shone onto the magnificent scene. Although the sea seemed calm, the people around us were panic-stricken. Our eyes wandered far into the distance to the horizon, where inextricable, rough, foamy waves rushed rapidly back to the shore. By now, everyone had evacuated and we were left staring in awe at the mammoth waves looming over us. Were we going to survive somehow?

Foos Abdulahi (14)
Hornsey School For Girls, London

Heat

I was walking through the arid land, my empty bucket weighing down on my head. It'd been two years since the sun's cruel rays first burnt my land, piercing my tender skin.

After an hour strolling north, I crashed onto the ground. The exhaustion was getting the best of me and signalled me to go home. My eyes burnt as dust flew into them. My throat grasped for any cool air it could find. I looked over my village, once busting with life, now barely living. Another day I'd failed. Another day with no water. We should have done better...

Kadija Mohamed (15)
Hornsey School For Girls, London

Surface: Deep Under

Do you ever get that feeling that something bad is about to happen? Well, I wish I'd listened to that feeling two weeks ago when it arose. Abandoned, betrayed, forgotten, I'm now trapped here, imprisoned like a criminal. I've always been interested in the deep blue sea, but never in my whole ten years did I ever think it would rise! Chaos took over. We were surrounded. People desperately threw themselves into the lifeboats, praying there would be enough space. However, when the last ship left without me, my heart sank like the Titanic. Now, will I ever escape?

Keeley Daniella O'Callaghan (12)
Hornsey School For Girls, London

The Unanswered Crisis

The streets ran with blood. There were crying mothers, screeching children and many more noises I really couldn't define. I thought, *is this what the world has really become?* The word 'nuclear' had become a word a two-year-old knew. The state of crisis that I suffered was unimaginable. The sky filled with fog that no one was able to see through. Then the bullets came, the running, the screaming, a noise that tingled my senses. I knew something was wrong, but I couldn't figure it out. I heard the roar of a jet. Suddenly, out of nowhere... blank.

Maryan Bashir Farah (13)
Hornsey School For Girls, London

Power

The volcano stood tall in front of Jacob. The magma below him bubbled like hot water heating up in a kettle. An immense guillotine of bleak smoke cut through the sky across the horizon. Jacob was terrified! This was something he'd never forget. His heart pounded painfully against his chest. His heart skipped a beat as the volcano roared with all its might. He felt squeezed like he was in a vice. Magma erupted out of the volcano and loomed ominously over the village. The nearby crater and plume of smoke was a menacing reminder of the volcano's awesome power...

Magdalena Peric (14)
Hornsey School For Girls, London

Tcf

It's been a year since my dad died. Mother was all I had. She chopped her finger last year whilst cooking. Consumed with agony and pain brought no comfort. The last words my father said to me were "T-C-F," which made no sense. One night I played the Ouija game in my room to try and contact my father. A wind of hesitation consumed me and brought tears to my eyes. The words 'T-C-F' were highlighted. Memories of my father zoomed past me and everything made perfect sense. 'T-C-F' stood for the chopped finger. I was living with a murderer...

Verdi Mbumba (13)
Hornsey School For Girls, London

Pestilence

Sickness engulfed the population like wildfire. Earth had turned into a deserted land. Black substances flowed out of the mouths of the people who'd fallen prey to this virus. I heard the cries of nocturnal creatures in the distance. My arms hung limply as I managed to run out of the building where the virus was manifesting within the people I loved. I stared, aghast, at the austere men in black robes concealing themselves around me. I plunged into a hole of uncertainty. Surely, there was something I could do. Or was there no more chance of survival for anyone?

Roqia Matin (14)
Hornsey School For Girls, London

Never Wish For Too Much...

The monstrous flood tore down everything that stood in its way, leaving millions of shards as if our broken hope had become visible. Its menacing teeth bit away at the unprotected ankles that were submerged in its glory. The shattered Stygian street lay below the turbid water, sickly green-brown like the river carrying the trash that usually adorned the sidewalk. The city had gorged itself on the floor and its skin had swelled and burst in places. Though the rain has now stopped, the air still feels damp and the clouds that brought this upon us are yet to depart...

Saadath Ali (15)
Hornsey School For Girls, London

Burnt

I woke up. My throat was parched, my eyes watered. A vulgar scent, harsh like vinegar, crawled through the small gap in the window. On the floor was an orange, bubbling, oozing horror. There, fluctuating in the middle of the acid, were strands of my baby sister's curly hair! Fear clawed at my throat, paralysing my body, stopping my breath. Without thinking, my arm plunged into thick liquid. Ignoring the vengeful pain, I grabbed my sister's arm. I turned her body over, bile rising up my throat. My sister's unseeing eyes gazed upwards. She was dead.

Ohemaa Blankson (15)

Hornsey School For Girls, London

Wave Of Dread

Screaming? My eyes widened. I rose up from bed. *Was it a dream?* Glaring out of the window, my dainty jaw dropped. An aquamarine blanket of water rose from the ocean, cloaking the entire sky! My legs trembled like a newborn fawn. Instantaneously, I grabbed my Swiss army knife and phone and leapt down the stairs and out the door. A gust of wind caressed my hair. One foot in front of the other, my weak but powerful legs ran like they never had before. My mother sent me a message, 'Oliver, I love you. Please make it somewhere safe'...

Atosa Juliet Mohammadian (13)
Hornsey School For Girls, London

Skiing Crisis!

It was a fresh, spring Saturday morning when it happened. When the sun hit the snow, it sparkled. The satisfying crunch of cold fresh snow under my feet warmed me. My first push from my ski poles set me off. My hair was blowing in the wind. Falling snow covered my goggles. It was perfect. I felt alive, like I could live forever! Suddenly, I fell off course onto a steep mountainside. I was stuck and stranded. I thought, *what can I do?* The snow under my skis fell. I saw snow falling towards me. "Avalanche..."

Millie Hoare (11)
Hornsey School For Girls, London

Plastic Monster

I had finally finished building my amazing sandcastle. I felt extremely dehydrated, so I reached deep down into my bag for a can of coke. Once I had finished gulping it down, I subconsciously scanned the area to check for humans and threw the can into the sea. I proudly waved it goodbye. I was living my best life... Until suddenly, an enormous creature made up of plastic rose from the sea, roaring raucously. My coke can was standing on top of it. It looked directly at me and started marching. My end had finally arrived...

Samina Ahmed (15)
Hornsey School For Girls, London

Unbearable Heat

The sand lay on the ground as I breathlessly dragged my feet across the dry land beneath. My eyes rested upon the piercing rays of the sun and I prayed for the night to briskly spread its heavy blanket over the sky. My vision blurred. I stumbled. Sweat painfully trickled down the sides of my face. I heavily collapsed onto my knees. My chest heaving rapidly and panting heavily, I struggled to find anything to quench my thirst. My fingers fumbled with the zips on my bag, desperately grasping onto the plastic bottle. I screamed in agony. It was empty...

Irem Kademlioglu (15)
Hornsey School For Girls, London

The End Of Humanity

Silence. The dark sky resembles my inevitable death looming before me. The zombie lurks outside. My thoughts are a deep dark well of sorrow. To my knowledge, I'm the last surviving human on Earth. Carefully, I steady myself as the overpowering stench of death cascades into my nose. On the verge of fainting, I rummage through my bag for my dagger. A swift movement catches my eye and I find the same zombie lying still with an arrow sticking out of its skull. No... it can't be! Trembling, I slowly turn to see two icy blue eyes boring into me...

Noora Younes (13)
Hornsey School For Girls, London

Gone

Bins were tipped over, rubbish everywhere. Thick fog filled the air and a little boy emerged from behind a piece of corrugated plastic. He looked terrified. He shouted out, but had to stop mid-sentence due to a sob that rose up inside him. He ran towards me, his eyes wide with fear. He reached out for help, for something to give him stability. My hand stretched out, offering him refuge. Just as he was about to make contact with me... Gone. The wind of another building hurricane had ripped him from existence. He was just gone. My own brother, gone.

Emily Marks (14)
Hornsey School For Girls, London

The Unknown

My name is Max Sag, but it doesn't matter what I'm called or what I write. It's not like anyone will live to read this. It's unknown. Everything is. No one knows why their families have vanished. No one knows anything, not even the cause of this chaos. The prime minister is gone. I've been able to locate a few friends, but that still doesn't change much... or anything at all. Imagine this, you are just fine living with your family in North London and then you wake up and find yourself with no choice but to arm yourself...

Khadidja Cheref (13)
Hornsey School For Girls, London

Burn

Lava! The volcano in Thailand had erupted, covering the entire area in hot bubbling lava. All she heard was the screams and shouts of the people in pain. Below her, she saw burnt bodies floating away with the lava. Her phone flickered as she saw the word 'news' appear. The entire population was being burnt to death! She had to help them. She broke the pipe, causing all the water from the tank to burst out, splashing onto her fellow citizens. Suddenly, she slipped and fell from the roof into the molten lava. She was burning in agony...

Jannat Ahmed (14)
Hornsey School For Girls, London

Melting

An outburst of a virus had broken out on the monotonous streets of London. The unexpected had come to strike. Civilians started to melt and effervesce until they became a puddle of their own soul. Bodies started to deluge the streets of London. Everybody could no longer move and they were swimming in a sea of their own. Those who ran had to run for miles. Come into contact with a melting human and your fingers would start to drip with every second. All was lost except for the buildings who witnessed this disappearing act of the human beings.

Syeda Nazifa Khatun (14)

Hornsey School For Girls, London

The Wildfire That Changed My Life Forever

It seemed like the world had ended. I felt like it was only me who'd survived the wildfire. I had lost everything, simply everything. We had been enjoying our day with the lush blue sky above us, the birds singing, the molten gold sun and the puffball white clouds drifting along their invisible road to an undiscovered place waiting to be discovered. My mum, my dad and me had been sitting having a picnic and then it came. A forest fire approached us! Now, I was the only one left after the catastrophe. I was left to search for shelter...

Venus Sanjeewa (2)
Hornsey School For Girls, London

When There Was No Life Left

I sat there full of regret, knowing I'd caused it all. But there was no turning back now. All I remembered were the lifeless bodies that could be seen in every direction after a massive nuclear bomb had destroyed so many lives. Everyone had known that their lives would end then and there. Yet, I had stood there as if it was a sensational performance. I truly knew I was in denial. Now, my life was finally over but not in the sense of being dead. Imagine knowing millions of people have died because of you, how would *you* feel?

Mischa Serugo (12)
Hornsey School For Girls, London

Gempa Bumi

I couldn't breathe. My heart felt like it was in my throat and the world around me smelled like gas. I groped around, trying to find someone, anyone. I was desperate. From behind me, I heard a cracking noise and my eyes flew open. I gasped. All around me, there was rubble and collapsed buildings. But the most shocking thing was the amount of pale lifeless bodies strewn on the floor. I realised I was biting my tongue so hard I drew blood. As the metallic taste of blood filled my mouth, I heard a groan, "Help me, Indah..."

Isobel Carter (11)
Hornsey School For Girls, London

The Silence Of The Skies

Stirring, I wake up. Silence. The foggy surroundings muffle the screams of the life around me as I sit up, groaning. The skies are grey with the memory of what's just happened. But the wave that just hit seems as though it has washed my mind out with it. Where am I? What's going on? As if in slow motion, a group of people rush towards me, lifting me onto a long wooden plank, taking me to safety. Safety? What even is safe after this? Is it when you feel secure, warm, comfortable. I don't know what safety is anymore.

Iva Shehu (13)
Hornsey School For Girls, London

Running Towards Evil

I run, hearing only my heartbeat beating like it's going to jump out of my chest and my two feet pounding against the dry mud. Blisters make it harder, but I don't stop. Out of the corner of my eye, I see the attor, claws so sharp they could slit you in half. It comes running towards me, making a terrifying shrieking sound. I duck down, take my arrow and throw it right through its neck. I stop, breathing hard. Hearing a deep laugh behind me, I turn around and there he is, staring at me with those black eyes...

Sheyda Shamshin Lalehiloo (13)
Hornsey School For Girls, London

The Curse Of The Tsunami

It was happening. It'd take us in and swallow us alive! I ran and ran, but it was getting closer. The temperature dropped. My feet were turning all sorts of colours. It rose up my body. I was as cold as the shivers that run down your spine when you face doom. My eyes roamed all over the place until they met the waves rushing towards us at maximum speed. We didn't know what to do! Palm trees and houses were now in different places, with innocent people dead. The monstrous tsunami had come for what it wanted...

Latifa Sheikh Wali (14)
Hornsey School For Girls, London

Luck Is Pain

I was soaked with water. I felt like a soggy biscuit, drenched, helpless. I had got to higher ground and, below me, I could see all the people being flung around like ice cubes bobbing up and down in the water. But the water was determined and there was no stopping it. It was the predator and we were its prey. Looking at the innocent people below me, I felt... what was it? Pity? Guilt? Whatever it was, it made me want to grab their hands and bring them to safety. But what could I do? Nothing, nothing at all.

Ami Marks (12)
Hornsey School For Girls, London

Taken

I remember waking up at 3:37am. I was boiling and couldn't sleep. I went to get some water, but when I turned the tap on, the water that was going into my glass was a sickly brownish yellow. That's when I knew I had to get out. With my heart thumping, I reached for my doorknob. I jumped back in pain, my fingers fleshy and red with marks on. Opening my door, I saw the terrifying sight of chaos! Black smoke filled my lungs, causing me to splutter. I saw my life flash before my eyes. What had I done?

Zubaida Chowdhury (15)
Hornsey School For Girls, London

The Wave

The ground shook. Suddenly, my feet gave way before me. Ten minutes ago, the beach was full of ecstatic people enjoying their holiday. But now, when I turned around, there was no one to be seen. Everyone had run away! I soon saw why... I looked at the horizon and I saw the most immense wave in the history of waves! To the eye, it looked to be 100 metres tall. I heard a sudden shriek of fear. This wasn't a scary dream, it was reality. I remembered my mum had been surfing in the sea. Where was she now?

Saffron Gardner (12)
Hornsey School For Girls, London

The End

The end of the world had come. My whole entire world was flashing in front of me. I lost everything. I had nothing to say, but I was strong. It felt like I was the only one who survived the tornado. It started with stormy weather which ended in disaster. The houses bounced everywhere and blood was the only thing I could see. I felt scared and homeless because all the city was destroyed. All were dead but I had survived the tornado. I had no food, no home, nothing but a photo of my dear lovely parents...

Silvia Hajdari (12)
Hornsey School For Girls, London

River Of Lava

I am in the forest and I can see the distant lava erupting. I try and escape. I have to run fast. I run to the door and all I can see is mist that is blinding my eyes. I pant and keep on panting. Suddenly, I hear a whoosh and I fall over. I try and get up, but I can't get up! Suddenly, I am whooshed into the river of lava and I try to survive but I can't do anything! I think, *I might die soon in this erupting volcano...*

Chloe Turner (12)
Hornsey School For Girls, London

A Race Against Time

I hear loud talking on the road below me. I am intrigued. I walk down and open my door. While walking out, my neighbour catches my eye and points over to the forest. Thick black smoke is pouring into the sky above. While scanning the ruins, I see something worse. A large, orange monster threatening our city! As it looms closer, worry takes over everyone's faces. As every second goes by, the city gets closer to a massive disaster...

Lola Meaden (15)
Hornsey School For Girls, London

A Fiery Dance

A veil of darkness swallowed the once pale blue sky. Fierce fire could be seen sneaking its way through the trees. Glowing embers leapt and twirled in the sky a fiery dance, twinkling like stars before cascading down to Earth. Houses turned into mazes of flames. The entire village burnt in a sea of red, yellow and orange. Screams tore through me like shards of glass. Desolate sobs echoed into the night. It was all my fault.

Rachel Little (14)
Hornsey School For Girls, London

The Storm

"Nineteen, twenty!" John said smugly.

"Oh, you win!" Serena whimpered.

"Go on, choose, truth or dare?"

"Truth!" she replied.

"Is it true it's all gone?" he whispered.

"Yes, it's true. We both saw it," Serena whispered.

"How did it start?"

"Remember?" she said. "The sky rumbled with rage, the clouds darkened. The wind howled, followed by screams. Flashes of lightning lit up the sky. We ran as fast as possible. We lost everything and everyone."

"Are we safe now?"John asked.

"Yes we are," Serena replied.

"Are you sure?" he insisted.

The sky rumbled with rage...

Simran Joshi (12)
Kingsbury High School, Kingsbury

Is She Dead Or Alive?

Her eyes opened wide. Lying on the floor, her legs were tired after all those miles of walking. She asked, "Are we there yet, Liam?"
"No, but nearly. Just a few miles left, Kaytlin," answered Liam.
She got up, acting as strong as she could. Limping through the snow, she tried to ignore the pain, her hands shivering. As she noticed the mountain in front of her, she jumped with excitement.
"Liam, we're here!" shouted Kaytlin
With no pain, she started climbing the mountain. Suddenly, snow tumbled down. Kaytlin wasn't aware. Kaytlin fell to the ground. Could Liam do anything?

Anjali Pradipcumar (13)
Kingsbury High School, Kingsbury

Albert Einstein Saves Earth

Aliens were abducting people on Earth. Vampires were biting people's heads off making blood spray out of them, turning the atmosphere red. Albert Einstein was thinking of a way to rescue everyone. He took his sword and dual pistols and joined the fight. The green being's flying ships sucked frightened people inside them. A vampire sucked a woman's soul out and sucked her blood. Albert got out his pistol and shot every vampire and alien. "Two plus two is four minus one that's three! Quick maths!"

A bright glow filled up the sky and flashed. Albert Einstein had saved humanity.

Nicole Shamloo (13)
Kingsbury High School, Kingsbury

Heatwave

The sky burnt red, the air was humid. The ground was so dry, the cracks were wide. Plants shrivelled, sweat trickled. Dying of thirst, but hunger came first. No matter, only heat. It was hard to defeat. Dehydrated, it was hated. Water on my bucket list, I had been waiting for that bliss. Would we ever defeat the constant heat? On the edge, the constantly heated weather.
"Chloe, the heat is nearly over!" Andrew rejoiced.
"No! The worst is yet to come!" Chloe shouted.
As the hot wind blew in their faces, they ran. The heatwave was not over...

Romaissa Ennasry (12)
Kingsbury High School, Kingsbury

The End

The day was clear, the centre was busy. No one saw the earthquake coming, breaking homes, destroying lives, creating destruction and losing humanity. The boy survived in the field. He loved playing there. It saved him from doom in the tower block. The grass provided a cushion for him.

He woke to the signs of the apocalypse. All the buildings around him were down, flames devoured the sky, everyone was dead! He entered the security post and noticed a survivor crouching with a saucepan.

"They are coming!" the survivor screamed. "The aliens are coming! The aliens will come for us..."

Maxim Pudlo (13)
Kingsbury High School, Kingsbury

Hurry

Dread, darkness, disaster - all I can remember. Everything is an endless void. The sensation of tears creeps up on me.

It was unexpected when the hurricane hit. Trees falling, houses destroyed, lives stolen even from the innocent. It all happened in the blink of an eye. I guess I was lucky.

Now, I'm trying to survive with no food, just water. If only I could go back and save my family... In front of me, I can observe colossal trees that have fallen. *Bash!* Another hurricane? I'd better hurry or my life will end, if it hasn't already...

Hams Youssef (13)
Kingsbury High School, Kingsbury

The Cracks

The cracks were expanding. It was the end.

"Will we make it?" whimpered Lucy.

I didn't want to lie. She looked at me, with her wide eyes, desperately wanting me to tell the truth. The cracks were getting bigger and bigger. The buildings in the distance were losing control and disintegrating. We didn't have much time left. I could see the horror in her eyes. Mother Nature had returned for round two! The wind gained power and pieces of rubble tumbled down.

"Don't look down, Lucy!" I exclaimed.

"What do you mean?"

In a split second, she was gone...

Deborah Brobbey (12)
Kingsbury High School, Kingsbury

Disaster Splits Race

After hearing the news, I was puzzled. Was I going to die? Suddenly, I heard people screaming, "It's an earthquake, help!"
I quickly packed a few things like my phone and food. I looked outside. Buildings were collapsing as if they were fainting humans, screaming. I could see the ground splitting as if everyone was being divided. That's what the people had wanted, categories, everyone in sections. Now it was happening. It felt like every race was separated, their wish was coming true. Fire. I smelt people burning. I wanted it to stop right that minute...

Sara Sayeed (13)
Kingsbury High School, Kingsbury

The Unknown Earthquake

I was sleeping when it happened. I was in a deep sleep but suddenly, I felt my bed shake. Instantly I thought *what is happening? Why is my bed shaking? reassuring myself not to panic,* I quickly ran downstairs. I searched for my parents, however, they were nowhere to be seen! I ran out of the house because it seemed like the most sensible thing to do...

It's a few weeks later and it has ended. Buildings are destroyed and people are dying due to lack of food and water. Nobody knows what caused the earthquake, even the smartest scientists...

Shahad Sharif (13)
Kingsbury High School, Kingsbury

Ever Running

Life was decent until the day it happened. We were passing The Shard and saw somebody shaking and mauling at something. We stopped. He was eating a human liver! We were shocked, not just by that, but by his face which was as broken as glass. He was horrified, desperate and lost. My dad took out his gun like he was unsure. We edged back, then the man jumped and bit someone! He said, "You started it, it's all your fault, your fault!"
The person who'd been bitten stopped shaking. His eyes were hungry and he ate everyone he saw...

Mujtaba Ahmad (13)
Kingsbury High School, Kingsbury

Calm Before The Storm

It came rushing towards the Earth with its fiery tail and hot face. It had one mission - crashing into Earth! It was humanity's last moments as all efforts to stop it were in vain. Everyone was silent, waiting for their inevitable demise. The humans terrified, the animals confused and the Earth nervous. Alarms screamed as the asteroid zoned in on the Earth. There was a fear in the air consuming the Earth. When the expected impact time came, nothing happened! The cloud of fear was replaced with a cloud of happiness. Strangely, it started raining metal with red eyes...

David Cyrus Bahrami (12)
Kingsbury High School, Kingsbury

Isolated And Almost Brain Dead

My shirt and hair stuck to my neck with sweat. The cold tap had long since been stopped by the government as it was reserved for hospitals. The ruthless sun beat down angrily on the metal of my shelter. My wooden home had burnt down three hours prior. Tongue dry, throat hoarse, I hadn't uttered a word in days. I crawled towards the pile of empty bottles strewn across the floor, searching for a single drop to ease my heavy breathing. Final breath, vision blurry, head pounding, dizzy, hallucinating. I collapsed to my knees. The heat was unbearable. I fell...

Sara Tillaih (13)
Kingsbury High School, Kingsbury

The Beginning

"We are not expecting anyone to survive this hurricane..."
I stared at my TV. I wasn't going to survive, I knew it! Still, I snatched my bag from my peg and ran to my room. I needed to escape. I stuffed my essentials in and I went out of the back door. The ground beneath my feet rumbled as the clouds towered over my head. I could hear the thunder in the distance. It was the beginning... The wild wind hit my face with a negative influence of coldness. As I ran, houses behind me collapsed, making deafening noises...

Sara Alexia Iordan (12)
Kingsbury High School, Kingsbury

Zombie Infections

In 2018, a young scientist called Bobby tried to make a cure to stop disease in America. If it worked, he would send the cure around the world. He tried it on a person, but it didn't work. It made the guy turn into a zombie! Bobby ran away and headed somewhere safe.

After thirty-four years, the world was infected with zombies and the only survivor was Bobby. He went to a mansion in Florida that none of the zombies knew about. Bobby went to get food and water at the abandoned shops. Suddenly, there was a zombie attack...

Vinusan Padmarasa (12)
Kingsbury High School, Kingsbury

The End Is Near

Dying. The world was coming to an end. Babies crying, dogs barking and women screeching. Hell had broken loose. Mother Nature had taken over. The trees had begun to fall and planes had started to spin out of control and crash into nearby buildings. It was 9/11 all over again! Tsunamis were everywhere. These combined with hurricanes was not the best combination. I felt helpless, scared, alone. All my friends had died from the catastrophe. All I had was myself. Was this really the place to be? Would I be better or surviving? Or would I be better off dead?

Kody Nembhard Dale (12)
Kingsbury High School, Kingsbury

The Unspoken Parts Of The World

Dreadful, disastrous, doom. I can't see anything but the swirl of menacing grey coming closer and closer. The thought of knowing that I could soon fall into an eternal sleep traumatises me. Every day, this is how life is now. People didn't care about this world of ours. Cars, factories, these were some of the things that created this shelter of intense warmth. We are now covered with a blanket of thick perspiring heat. Fewer people are able to possess their lives. The world is about to end and I think I might be the only one still surviving...

Avni Kiran Hirani (12)
Kingsbury High School, Kingsbury

Hope, Prey, Survive

I was a policeman stationed in California. Suddenly, the Earth shook violently. The temperature rose. Molten lava exploded from the tip of a nearby volcano! The stray ash was painted across my face. I began to wheeze heavily. I felt a sharp pain. Tiny pieces of debris invaded my injured hand. I fled to an office block and rushed five stories up. The lava chased me! I bandaged my hand. I used my walkie-talkie to call for help. Unexpectedly, the building started to vibrate and the windows shattered. I realised I was trapped with the lava still rising...

Vanajan Subaskaran (13)
Kingsbury High School, Kingsbury

Markle's Cave

Markle lived in snowy Alaska. There was a great haunted cave nearby, so he decided to venture into it.

When he arrived, he caught a glimpse of a tall figure peeking out. He went in to see what it was. Unfortunately, a brutal avalanche occurred. Markle could not escape, so he went deeper into the suspicious cave to find out what had lured him in. There was a towering silhouette coming towards him! Markle's scream was heard from far away. Only his bloody head was found. This story has been passed on for generations. Will you pass it on to?

Nour Jaafar (13)
Kingsbury High School, Kingsbury

The Mouse Meat

Below a mountain, a couple were on a date. They were only sixteen. Suddenly, an avalanche happened! They survived the avalanche somehow, but they only had a packet of biscuits, a phone and a knife. Martha was stuck and they ran out of food. It was freezing! At that moment, James gave Martha some mouse meat he said he'd found. Martha ate it with disgust. James gave the mouse meat to her until the rescuers came. Martha survived. James passed away. The mouse meat was his flesh! After Martha knew about it, she cried for him and never got married.

Suxin He (13)
Kingsbury High School, Kingsbury

The End Of The Human Era

December 13th 4213. An earthquake is bashing through the Earth's surface. There are only a few humans still surviving. Mother Nature is surviving well. Plants are growing on broken buildings. Building by building, everything's falling apart. Mutated animals walk towards me. A mutated wolf pounces and scratches me badly. I grab it and rip it apart. I swiftly go towards the nearest shelter. The stormy sky starts to rain with heavy thunder and lightning. The lightning strikes down in front of me. The rain starts to make the place flood...

Zaid Tahir (12)
Kingsbury High School, Kingsbury

The Flood

Me, my family and my friends are shopping like normal. My mum tells me to get juice, so I go. As I'm in a good mood, I start to skip around. Suddenly, as I jump, I feel cold water hit me. I look up, suspecting nothing but a leak in the roof. Suddenly, a heap of water splashes the whole shop - a flood! At this point, I'm worried, scared and I'm trying to find my family and friends. I finally see them and go to them.

"Where's Mum?" I ask.

I can see a body floating. It's my mum...

Ayanna Grant-Wright (13)

Kingsbury High School, Kingsbury

Nightmare Come True!

A terrible day occurred. I was standing on top of a strong building. I saw my nightmare- a tsunami! My heart skipped a beat. I grabbed my microphone and said, "Everyone, get to the tallest building!"
I put the emergency alarm on. As they ran, the tsunami came closer and closer. It took out a few people. It was bad! I called to my friends to come upstairs. It was the first day of my job with my two friends. We had all been excited. I didn't know where they were now though. I hoped they were safe...

Dhea Kerai (12)
Kingsbury High School, Kingsbury

The Catastrophe Of The Micro-Chips

I know all about it...

I was at school and I forgot my pencil case in the science lab. As I went closer, I heard something that chilled my blood - Mr Sam planning to create a microchip that could slowly kill victims! He said, "I will put this in all food products."

I first thought it was a prank to fool someone, but then the day came when he actually put the microchips in all food products. I saw it all with my bewildered eyes. I tried to warn everyone but it was too late. What will happen now?

Akshay Pradipcumar (13)
Kingsbury High School, Kingsbury

I Should Die To Survive

The England we knew was gone. We were in the hands of the corrupted. There we were, chained up at the side of the road like dogs. No freedom. If we thought about stepping over the line, the repercussions would be devastating. Our primal instincts overcame us. Everyone was against the tragic world. It was clear how a fire raged in everyone's eyes; the torment of fear, the tsunami of fury. I'd lost everything. Nothing and no one to love and live for. Nothing to care for either. I have no reason to live. I had to die to survive...

Kiran Sivakumar (13)
Kingsbury High School, Kingsbury

The Death Of A Neighbour

Reader, my name is Kai. I'm twenty-four. When you read this, I'll be in hospital...

My alarm blared into my ears. I smelt an extreme burning smell. I got ready and ran outside as fast as a bullet. My neighbour's home was on fire! It was abominable. Without thinking, I ran inside. I was suffocating! The temperature was as overwhelming as the sun's surface. I heard a voice, "Help!"

Once I'd found him, he was dead. My body was shaking and I was dripping gallons of sweat. The ambulance came rapidly.

Anoj Roy (12)
Kingsbury High School, Kingsbury

A Dream?

Me and my friends are trying to get out. We are stuck inside the school. The door lock is stuck! We are freezing because someone left all of the taps on and blocked the sinkholes where the water goes. The water is getting higher and higher! We are panicking. After that, we drown.
Suddenly, I wake up like it was all a nightmare! I thought it was real! There are tears sliding down my cheek. When I get to school. I will tell my friends, but I'm still wondering why I woke up soaking wet and freezing...

Sora Sherif (13)
Kingsbury High School, Kingsbury

Stone Cold

It happened so suddenly. I felt so hollow. Everything inside me was like an endless void. Nobody saw it coming except me. I looked out the stone-cold window and a sensation of fear devoured me. They were motionless. Bodies lay on the ground, some half-burnt. As tears blurred my vision, I took one last look at my home before I looked away. The virus had come, the cold and distressing virus. I set out. I had to get away from everything, isolate myself. I couldn't get more isolated than the island cabin. I took a deep breath...

Diya Khetani (13)
Kingsbury High School, Kingsbury

Hurricane Leslie

One day, Ben was having a usual day until he watched the weather forecast. It showed that Hurricane Leslie was on its way! He started to panic, but he remembered that all he had to do was pack a survival kit. He started packing. He packed tinned food and also water and medicine. He finished packing in the nick of time. He ran to his basement with everything he needed and stayed there with his phone, watching to see when it said it was over. Ben could hear the strong winds coming from outside. He stayed there until it stopped.

Abderrahime Hamadache (13)
Kingsbury High School, Kingsbury

Fire Is Hell

One early morning, life changed. Nature was angry, burning everything it caught in its sharp red-hot jaws, leaving behind... nothing. So I had to flee. I could smell the burning hot flames filled with dark ash. I got everything I could find, started my car and left. A pain like never before struck me. The fire was all around me! I thought I would die. I prayed and prayed to God and he listened to me. I was rescued! The sky was filled with scorching ash while I was lifted above the ground. I was rescued by a helicopter!

Theodor Purav (12)
Kingsbury High School, Kingsbury

In The Eye Of The Hurricane

My feet trembled as I walked. The sand beneath my feet crawled through the gaps of my toes as though it was running from something, something malignant. Something flashed before my eyes - a blast of wind and sand. It happened again. A flash of light brown swept past my face. It continued to happen. A clump of sand was blown by the ferocious wind, creating a whirlwind. It engorged and moved towards me. I made a run for it, but my bandage got caught in the bush. It was coming closer and closer. It got me...

Nazifa Ahmed (13)
Kingsbury High School, Kingsbury

Everything Goes Down With The Tower

"I have enough money," said Bargo.

He went up to the man and the man took the money and gave him a ticket. Bargo went into the elevator and he was excited and couldn't believe his dream was becoming a reality! He got up and took out his telescope. He could see all of Paris. Then the Eiffel Tower started to shake and he realised it was an earthquake! The supports holding the tower went plummeting to their doom into the crack of the earthquake along with Bargo! He knew it was over now...

Hussainali Sachoo (12)
Kingsbury High School, Kingsbury

Deadliest

People were running from a deadly wildfire. It was hotter than a volcano. The smoke was toxic. If you had one sniff, you would die. People were evacuating California. It was dangerous! People died in it. The wildlife lasted for four days.

A few days later, when people had just settled into their homes again, there was a loud bang. It was a hurricane! Everyone looked on the news. The speed was 500 miles per hour and it was the deadliest hurricane the world had ever seen...

Nyal Hirani (13)
Kingsbury High School, Kingsbury

The School Lockdown

I was at school in the bathroom. Then, all of a sudden, the alarm went off. It was saying, "Lockdown! Please lock all the windows and doors."
I wasn't near any classrooms, so I locked myself in the bathroom stall and I was shaking like a leaf. *Bang!* The door burst open and the person held a gun up to my head! Then, a teacher tackled him to the ground. I ran as fast as a cheetah to a classroom and locked it. But then, I heard a sound that I never wanted to hear. A gunshot...

Courtney Martindale (13)
Kingsbury High School, Kingsbury

Prey

I knew it was coming... the end. All over the news, world hunger, deaths increasing, finding loved ones dead. A simple problem with a hard solution. We were too many people with too little food. Every morning, I woke up with a sick feeling in my stomach. I had to get some food, all I had was a piece of bread. I left the house to search. *Bang!* I spun around to see a lady, my sister! The bullet hole burnt my flesh and soul. The last thing I saw was her taking the bread. Why would she?

Aminulla Nazari (12)
Kingsbury High School, Kingsbury

Nothing To Live For

The cold air danced around me as I stepped outside. All of a sudden, I heard wailing sounds, almost as if a siren was going off. I became nervous, so I removed my woolly hat to see if I was just hearing things. I wasn't. An old alarm used in WW2 had been revived. It meant that there was a bombing! Run! All above me, there were sparks flying in the sky. The sparks were planes on fire! I got up. I knew there was no point in saving myself. I had nothing to live for...

Muhammad Abdulkadir Awes (13)
Kingsbury High School, Kingsbury

Extinction

It started out like this, people screaming, panicking and crying for their lost loved ones. Fire was spreading everywhere, all caused by the meteors. The meteors kept on hitting the building I was in, shattering it like a piece of glass. I saw a radio beside me. I was surprised it still worked. I turned it on. It said the world was going to end...

Rahul D'Souza (13)
Kingsbury High School, Kingsbury

The Storm Of Fire

I woke to thunder and echoing booms that rang in my ears, ricocheting in my brain and rattling my thoughts so I couldn't think straight. The power went out, the sky darkened and then the world was filled with fire. Ash snaked across the horizon, unstoppable, cutting scars into the city. Fire spat, leaping for joy at its freedom from the confines of stone. I flung myself outside, desperately hunting for fresh air, my skin scarred at the touch of each smouldering snowflake. Billowing smoke consumed everything. The darkness reached out its claws and delivered me to Satan's greedy hands.

Emily O'Grady (15)
Nower Hill High School, Pinner

My Turn

They can hear me before they see me. A low growl, a swelling roar. Thick, black dust cloaks my approach and swallows all who try to thwart me. Feeble, weak, it's futile. I thunder along my path of destruction, brushing away another skyscraper with a wave of my hand. Their pain thrills me. Their desperation provokes me. Another step forward splits the ground beneath my feet as my face is split with a grin. The terror is ripe. My fingers itch to ruin. With a final snarl, I stretch them out, reaching for those fragile, lost souls. It's my turn.

Rachel Louise Tobin (15)
Nower Hill High School, Pinner

Rebel

It was like a furnace. The door unyielding, meaning an endless baking session was unleashed upon us. I clawed at the latch, trying to open the windows, hoping for at least one breath of cool air, but I ended up receiving a gust of horrid oppressiveness. It had reached the point where the beads of sweat that rolled down my neck evaporated by the time they reached my shoulders. The forces of life inside my body fought an infinite battle against the fiery, ferocious flames. It started to shrivel up, the ball that kept us alive, Earth...

Abishah Sooriyakumar (15)
Nower Hill High School, Pinner

What A Wonderful World

Andrew's ears were ringing obstreperously now the overwhelming chaos had been silenced. It distracted him enough to force himself onto his feet, despite the agonising throbbing in his leg. Determination was written across his ashen face as he looked ahead. A wave, a colossal wall of raging water was crashing towards him, obliterating everything in its path, swallowing it in tempestuous anger. It was advancing at an alarmingly rapid pace, getting bigger and bigger. Andrew realised with a mixture of fear and valour that this wasn't just a wave, it was the fifth phase of Earth's destruction. The fifth wave...

Ruby Durack Lawlor (13)
St Anne's Catholic High School For Girls, Palmers Green

The World Before Yours

Before your world, there was another universe, but this universe was split into three factions: the Norsemen, the Grecians and the Romanics. The leaders of these factions were Odin, Zeus and Jupiter. Although this universe seemed peaceful, these three factions were at war. And when three gods battle, it doesn't end well. You see, if these gods combined their power, it would destroy the universe from the inside out, therefore forming a new universe! But the gods didn't listen to me! I mean, why would you listen to an oracle? It's not like the Big Bang will destroy us...

Hannah Maria McGrath-Becerra (12)
St Anne's Catholic High School For Girls, Palmers Green

The Ugly Truth

It's the end of the world as we know it. The government is hiding more than we know. It's 2222 and, if you're reading this, things have gone horribly wrong. I'm on my way to the White House and when I get there, I'm going to prove what the government is doing.

I arrive and sneak through a hidden vent. When I clamber out, I can't believe what I see. Everything I need to prove what they are doing here! But this is too easy... Someone's here! They're armed and coming towards me. You must know! No, it's *them...*

Grace Corcoran (12)

St Anne's Catholic High School For Girls, Palmers Green

Mission Catastrophe

It is the end of the world as we know it and our whole system is ruined!
"Lucy!" Mum calls. "Get to the panic room!"
I realise that another catastrophe has probably come to destroy us. They are taking over the world! A catastrophe is a (stupid) piece of machinery that has destroyed our government and country! I have made it my duty to save the world. Unfortunately, it isn't going well since I'm in a panic room trying my hardest not to scream. But I have accomplices to help. My life is a mission catastrophe...

Maliha Newman (12)
St Anne's Catholic High School For Girls, Palmers Green

The Vision

"It's the end of the world as we know it!" Falcon said, staring out the window. His sister gave him a look. "It wasn't a dream," he said. "It was a vision." Last night, Falcon had had a dream that he was a spy and was given a mission to save the world, but it went terribly wrong. He noticed a man in a black suit. "That's the man from the dream!" he yelled. "The one who grabbed me!" In his dream, Falcon was about to save the world when a man grabbed him and threw him off a building...

Caitlin Kitty MacLaren (11)
St Anne's Catholic High School For Girls, Palmers Green

The Unknown

It was the end of the world as she knew it. The people of the town were freaking out and the dogs were barking. Alex's long, wavy, brown hair blew in the wind as she hoverboarded over the town of terrified people. What was she going to do? Those things were taking over and she could do nothing about it! She watched in despair as she saw the whole town crumble to pieces. Was there *anything* she could do? Suddenly, the shadow of a man appeared. It was her father! But the thing was, her father was already dead...

Rhianna Travasso (11)
St Anne's Catholic High School For Girls, Palmers Green

The End Of The World

The world as we knew it was ending. The deafening sound of agony echoed across the land. It had been so long since I'd heard a laugh. A crystal-clear teardrop cascaded down my pink, rosy cheeks as I glanced at the horror of my desecrated home. I knew I had to run away, but where I'd end up... that was another story. I ran and ran but there was no escape. Soldiers and police were guarding the area. I didn't know exactly when this horrible time would end, but what I did know was that it wouldn't be soon...

Grace Joan Hanrahan (12)
St Anne's Catholic High School For Girls, Palmers Green

A Piece Of Mind

July 13th 2118

Dear diary,

Mum and Dad just called Quinn and me into the living room to discuss 'something important'. We went in, they turned on the TV and we listened in dead silence as the news reporter spoke. She looked very melancholic and spoke slowly and clearly. Most of it I couldn't understand, partly because I couldn't wrap my head around the fact that the world was going to split in half over the next couple of hours and that we should keep family close. Quinn started crying, we all hugged. I knew this was the end...

Cara Kirsten Ehrenreich (12)

St Catherine's School, Twickenham

The Last

When the catastrophe happened, I was up in space. From my view, Earth was being scrunched up like a ball of paper. Suddenly, fire sprang up; flames licked life away with its burning touch. When the fire had stopped, I directed the rocket towards Earth and stepped out. I was the only survivor, the only human left. There was no point in life anymore. I thought the world had given up but it had one last thing inside it. An explosion sounded. The world shook. I was blown back. Falling on the ground, the last human died - me.

Eleanor Rowbottom (11)
St Catherine's School, Twickenham

The Mega-Apocalyptic Disas-Trophe

The luminescent, green safety beacon laboured through the darkness to shine its blessed light. It was safe. To abandon the rugged, run-down shelter, we pushed up the artificial grass, escaping the mounds of mud, soil and dirt encasing us in our underground abode. Cheers rang through Earth, but this was only the beginning. Faces creased with concern. Eyebrows knotted with apprehension. The apocalyptic catastrophe had dwarfed and weakened, allowing fatalities and casualties to emerge from hiding. It was not over. Not yet. The world was doomed to crumble to its demise. Unless the universe was saved, the end was coming...

Ayaana Chowdhury (11)
St Paul's Catholic College, Sunbury-On-Thames

Chaos In A Nutshell

This time, the war was personal. Earthquakes and zombies surrounded the area. Our home planet was looking like a gigantic ball of flames. Everyone's screams got louder as it reached level 4 of the unnatural disaster. As slowly as a sloth, the Earth's sphere started crumbling into two halves. The heat from Earth's core turned my hands into crisp potatoes quicker than the speed of light. I crawled weakly as the zombies grew and grew, attempting to turn me into sausage meat. I took one last look at the brilliant sun, then my eyes went black.

Oluwadamilare Ryan Osikoya (11)

St Paul's Catholic College, Sunbury-On-Thames

Dare You Stand?

Stretched tears of the now solemn Earth cascaded endlessly upon the arid surface, she engulfed us in a blanket of blue. A sunken stitch stabbed my fragile side but I continued darting through the gnarled wilderness, bewildered. Imminently, she stealthily began to rise like a spider climbing a wall. Vulnerable, alone, the tempest sensed this too, the wind began to roar - a deafening roar - whilst Earth was cradled in her arms. No illumination from the sun, instantaneously, my heart froze. With bulging eyes, I was blinded by Mother Nature.

Kathryn Whetter (12)
St Paul's Catholic College, Sunbury-On-Thames

Grace

The ground began to shake, a thick, black smoke formed above us. I glanced down to see a crack in the ground charging towards me. I ran to what I thought would be higher ground. My heart was beating so fast, I thought it would pop out of my chest! *Wait, thick, black smoke, rumbles in the ground, could this be the biggest disaster ever? Is the world ending?*

"Grace!" someone shouted. I turned but I couldn't see anyone. The thick, black smoke started suffocating me, I couldn't breathe...

Neelia Nandkoomar (11)
St Paul's Catholic College, Sunbury-On-Thames

Day Six: I Need Somebody

Alone, eerie silences rang through my ears. Where did he go? Why did he leave me? All alone, standing in the dilapidated world I once called home. No voices, no happiness, no will to live without him. Emptiness was all I felt, I had no desire to care for myself. I stood on the surface of the empty world, cautiously hiding with my gas mask behind the remains of a rotting bush. The stench of misery filled my heart. As I realised my father may be gone, my faith lost its meaning...

Sarah Tarafdar (13)
St Paul's Catholic College, Sunbury-On-Thames

Landscapes Of Ash

As deafening silence surrounded him, the man looked around and rubbed his eyes to adjust to the artificial light around him. He realised a blue patient gown was thrown onto him earlier as he got up and started walking. Past the blue curtains, there was a woman dressed in white who compelled him to stay, but he didn't. He practically ran but he still heard the woman's pleas. "Don't go!"

A few corridors later, there it was. A beautifully-lit double door. He pushed until it opened. Landscapes of grey ash appeared before him. It was true, he'd just missed Armageddon.

Dawid P Sokolowski (15)

The Douay Martyrs Catholic Secondary School, Ickenham

Behind The Flames

He was safe now but dreaded thoughts plagued his mind. Blinding blazes devoured the slowly disintegrating wood, crawling up the buildings like a beast to its prey. It was peaceful now. However, the shrills were ringing in his ears. Flames angrily roared. The crashes of heavy beams collided with blasts of smashing glass. He took a shaky breath, inhaling the crisp air that had been cut off moments before. The acrid mixture of soot and smoke had attacked his lungs, which made the nauseous feeling climb up his throat. It was hard to remind himself that he was safe now.

Daya Sian (15)
The Douay Martyrs Catholic Secondary School, Ickenham

The Cerulean Waters

The hail sprinted across the promenade like it was never going to leave. The seas roared as they climbed upon the banks, through the buildings and onto the courtyards. A little girl stood, her eyes fixated on the water. Dainty, innocent, in the midst of the bellows, the sea's screams struck the air. A cerulean wave charged towards the tiny figure, lashing at her feet. As the substance rose, her hair grew darker and her eyes dimmed. A hand fumbled. The wave grabbed her tightly as her delicate body was held up. Cobalt flashes reflected. Assistance was coming...

Caoimhe Hoyle (14)
The Douay Martyrs Catholic Secondary School, Ickenham

Horror

I shuddered in horror as my house was engulfed by hungry flames. I was covered in scorching ash, but inside, I was cold. I left my brother's limp body in the house. His soul had long been walking in the gardens high above, along with the others who hadn't survived the greatest catastrophe Earth had ever experienced. There wasn't anything I could do, nobody left to warn. The ground under me trembled again. Fear paralysed me. It wasn't as strong as last time, yet I was cowering. I felt dead myself. The fragile island of my sanity crumbled beneath me...

Urszula Jakobec (11)
The Heathland School, Hounslow

Disasters

"Mum? Dad? Where are you?" whispered Abigail. She ran to Arianna and Anna, her sisters. "Did you hear that? It sounded like an explosion."
"What?" shouted Ariana.
"I don't care!" yelled Anna.
"Look outside," whispered Abigail.
"Oh my, we have to leave. Come on! I don't want to die."
They left while seeing bright, scorching lava coming closer and closer by the second. The lava came and swept Abigail away. "Sis!" shouted Arianna. "Bye, my dear sister!" Just then, bloody, scary figures emerged from the distance while the lava surrounded them...

Maithili Patel (11)
Villiers High School, Southall

The Mystery Of The Mysterious Land

There I was, standing despondently as I could see the darkness conquering the light. There was nothing I could do but wait for a day where I'd be rescued from this deserted place.

I was fearless, I was going on an adventure. At least, that's what I thought. I was going to 'zone dangereuse'. It was in French so I couldn't understand it. It was night-time so I couldn't see much.

After a few hours, I went to sleep. Suddenly, the whole building started vibrating and the exit collapsed. I couldn't escape! This was the worst holiday I'd ever had...

Maverick Anushk Fernandes (12)
Villiers High School, Southall

Watered To The Ground

Thanks to the almighty, a few others and I survived mass death caused by the flood. We were able to escape from the demolition. There was devastated life, trees, cattle, damaged roads, bridges and properties, all floating. The calm nature took on an unbearable form of continuous precipitation and Antarctica was melting. People were forced to leave their homes and normal life was disrupted. We managed to survive the violent destruction. It was not easy but worth the hard work. We got together on the highest mountain in Chile and prayed to Mother Nature. She responded by healing Earth.

Bedanta Mukhopadhay (11)
Villiers High School, Southall

Trapped

Desperately, he scurried for cover from the disaster that sounded like a roar of a lion. The avalanche was leaving nothing in its path, destroying gorgeous greenery like the Plague. Yahweh could not believe his eyes. He felt as if they were devilishly deceiving him. The innocent boy sprinted and sprinted from his heavenly homeland. He was carrying a bucket alongside him.

All of a sudden, his journey was put to a pause, he was blocked by slippery snow. Yahweh grabbed the bucket, dug into the ice and positioned it behind him but little did he know, he was trapped...

Haidar Ali Zahir (12)
Villiers High School, Southall

The Alien Apocalypse

Tom is battling a husk. They are undoubtedly dangerous. One wrong move could cause severe consequences. Tom is fatigued and cannot stand up. Earth has been taken over by husks. They are generating pain towards humans. Their plan is to overrule humans and take the world for themselves. The sky howls and lightning strikes. Tom punches the husk, but it leaps on him. Its long nails move down his chest. The wounds are deep and cause Tom to collapse. The husk walks up to him. He takes Tom's sword and holds it to this chest. Suddenly, the husk drops backwards...

Daud Chaudhry (12)
Villiers High School, Southall

His Vision

Constant guilt hung over him throughout his years, it followed him into his daily actions and darkest points. It loomed over him like a dark cloud on a summer's day, always there, yet never in place. His name was a mere whisper in the wind, dust floating aimlessly without a destination, a melody without a purpose or end. He walked through the wasteland to find a vial of green, its glass was reminiscent of the infection that had spread. Bringing it to his mouth, he let the burning liquid travel down his throat, darkness enveloping his vision...

Safa Noor Aurangzaib (13)
Villiers High School, Southall

The End

It was a normal day, there was a flood like usual. Where I lived, there was always floods. I turned the TV on and checked when the floods would end, but it said that there were floods everywhere. My heart froze with fear. I remembered that this had happened before, the time the world almost ended, but this was different...

After a few days, a heatwave hit us but the floods still didn't go. My face was sweating while my feet were frozen. The human population started to decrease. Scientists started working together but would it be enough?

Mohammad Abbasi (11)
Villiers High School, Southall

Me, Myself And I

Facing outwards, I could see holograms of my self. I thought that I was crazy. I'd woken up on top of a thick, fluffy blanket of snow but there were splatters of red. The mountain that had recently sliced, devoured a chunk of my toe, the sight scarring my eyes. Crying out blood, a mysterious shadow sat still beneath my feet. Slowly, I looked up. My neck clicked like snapped oak wood. My lips quivered with fear and my eyes began to sink. The shadow came closer and closer. A voice croaked, "Help me..." His eyes flared bright green...

Abdulhakeem Fazaldin (12)
Villiers High School, Southall

After Earth

The year was 2049. War had raged, during which Husk broke out. Husk was a disease that could turn you into a lethal, bloodthirsty zombie. A scientist had attempted to create a serum that could stop Husk from infecting the brain, it had been unsuccessful, which was odd considering he created it. Tracer was one of the lucky, uninfected ones. It was a mystery how he remained undetected from the husks, so much so that he questioned the realness of it all. That is until he awoke to the smell of burning embers and a husk standing over him...

Jaiden Rehinsi (12)
Villiers High School, Southall

Over

The wind howled like a horror movie. I could barely see as my hair was thrashing violently across my face. Surrounded by nothing except the ghastly wind, high above, the towering trees swayed to and fro. *Crash!* I lept back as I stared at the shattered pieces of glass. Breathlessly, I stood, trying to hold back my tears. A bitter taste of dust entered my mouth as I thought of my beloved family. There wasn't going to be a single house existing after this thunderous hurricane. My life was completely over...

Hasviini Mahathevan (12)
Villiers High School, Southall

Just A Peek

A bit of light managed to escape the speckled plane caused by the mobile rubble. Five days and five nights, waiting, wishing for this madness to end. The brutal silence of the outside world was enough to drive one mad. The unknown was a curse. In this sewer, time was just a concept that you could never grasp. After the news of the earthquake, the world was meagre, interaction even more so. The curiosity inside me raged. I had to take a peek. I had to, it was the only way. *Click!* I opened the caged cover...

Aparna Sunil (13)
Villiers High School, Southall

The Lost War

The day is finally here. The day of conclusion, the day everyone's been waiting for. It is the day of the war. The day of death. *Bang!* goes the shutters of my house from the force of bombs. It is so strong. It is terrifying, absolutely terrifying. Men, women and children are suffering. I run for my life with my family of three. I run until I turn to see nobody behind me. "Where are they?" I question myself. A bomb fiercely explodes right in front of me, I fall to wake up strongly weak...

Akshaja Thangeswaran (12)
Villiers High School, Southall

Am I The Last Person Alive?

I finally decided to come out of the sewers. It was horrible, there were dead bodies everywhere. I couldn't even ask anyone for help because I could not see anyone, all I could see was smoky fog. I got scared, so I started running around to see if anyone was alive. I couldn't find one person alive. I fell down onto my knees and started crying. I didn't know how this happened, had the aliens attacked us? This was it, the end of the world. Was I the last person alive on Earth or was there more?

Renaiza Rodrigues (12)
Villiers High School, Southall

The Extreme Earthquake

On a disastrous, depressing day, I was extremely traumatised by the horrifying earthquake. My eyes were panicking as I saw the destroyed homes. My heart was pounding rapidly like a clock ticking. As I saw dead people, tears poured down like a puddle. Suddenly, during the earthquake, a harsh tsunami came, killing thousands of people. I ran for my life, my body shivering. As the water splashed onto me, I could hear rattling and crashing. As I closed my eyes, I could feel the wind, then it went black...

Mathumigaa Kugatheesan (12)
Villiers High School, Southall

The Great Eruption

I hear screaming. Suddenly, I turn around to see everyone running towards me. My heart sinks, seeing the volcano erupting. The crowd of people are absolutely terrified! In front of my eyes, I can see dead bodies. At this point, I think I'm going to die. I quickly run towards my house and grab a few things. My mission is to pass the horrifying volcano to survive. The only question that comes to my mind is, *am I going to be able to survive?* I run past the volcano. I nearly make it...

Kimpreet Gherra (13)
Villiers High School, Southall

Cataclysm

There was a tsunami. It started on the beach, thirty metres high on Boxing Day. This tsunami flooded communities along the coasts of the Indian Ocean. It killed more than 200,000 people. I was in the flood but I survived and went to the nearest mountain. As I was going to the mountain, I found my family in a car. They were also going to the mountain so I got into the car.

We reached the mountain. My brother pointed to our dog, who was stuck in the flood. This major tsunami cost us a lot.

Harsh Hiteshkumar (13)
Villiers High School, Southall

Drowning In Water

My heart sank. The news had just informed me of a dangerous flood that had caused millions of deaths in the southwest of London and it was heading my way. Soon, gushes of water would cover the streets. I was terrified. Since my sister had just gone to the library and wasn't picking up her phone, I ran outside to find her and bring her home, but that wasn't a good idea. The dirty water covering the streets was full of furniture. I soon realised that I had made a big mistake...

Sukhmanpreet Kaur (12)
Villiers High School, Southall

The Unexpected Flood

Out of nowhere came an extreme, unexpected flood. I heard a lot of water and that's when I noticed it had washed everything in my house away. I ran away before the cold, filthy water could touch me but it was too late. There was no escaping this. The only thing that would help was going underground. Five survivors came underground with me, two separated and the other three stayed with me.

Later, they had disappeared, then all I heard was three people screaming...

Sukhraj Singh Nagra (12)
Villiers High School, Southall

The Earthquake

One day, Mark was on the porch sitting when his mum called him to look at the news. Mark was shocked after looking, an earthquake was going to happen within hours.

Mark was sitting down watching the TV when the floor started to shake. Mark had started to run faster than ever before. He was looking at a sight no one would like to see. Blood was splattered all over the porch. A fiery ball started to move, then it split in half. Ten ugly creatures came out screeching...

Rishiban Rahuban (11)
Villiers High School, Southall

Chunks Of Snow

I was skiing down a mountain. When I reached the bottom, I saw a few chunks of snow falling. Without warning, those chunks became larger. I started to head back when a large mass of snow slid towards me. I couldn't believe my eyes! It took me a couple of seconds to realise what was happening. The mass of snow was charging at me at a speed of 80mph. I skied as fast as I could. I was racing away from the snow. I feared for my life, then I lost my balance and tripped...

Pawandeep Singh Kapoor (13)
Villiers High School, Southall

Die Or Survive...

All I had was a Swiss army knife. Luckily, I saved one of my friends. We were on the hunt for some land. Ever since Jupiter came spiralling and crashing into Earth, the Earth had been at stake. We were running from the lava flow. As we were running, giant boulders came down and hit the ground between me and Anas. The ground split and another small boulder fell onto Anas' leg. I was safe but Anas was in great danger. Lava was behind him. I couldn't help him...

Saran Kirupakaran (13)
Villiers High School, Southall

Nuclear Danger And Abdi Ranger

My past has been a disaster. I've seen many things I can't remove from my head. They haunt me to this day. I've gained a gift from the bomb that was beyond human creation. My name is Adbi Ranger. It was a normal day when all of a sudden, the TV changed channels and went to the news. My mum was in shock, the news was saying there was a bomb coming.

It went off, a shiver went through my body, then I was able to teleport to capture the villain!

Anas Jirow (12)
Villiers High School, Southall

The Volcano Death

I went to Spain and I saw a volcano. I saw houses surrounding and wondered, *what if it explodes?* My thoughts came true. I walked nearer and it exploded but not with lava, it was a monster, a lava monster! "Run!"

After a while, the monster was going somewhere away from me. I then remembered what my grandad told me. He said, "Whenever a volcano erupts, lava monsters will hatch out so you must run."

So, I ran for my life...

Himesh Vijai Valgi (11)
Villiers High School, Southall

Mission Catastrophe: UFO

As it is about to strike, I sense death and chaos. I can feel goosebumps all over me as it strikes. Something supernatural, huge and amazing. It is a UFO! I can hear screaming and killing. I can see death and destruction. What is happening and how did everything end up like this? People are running. Should I run? "Someone help me!" I think they are after me. I run and close my eyes. The next thing I see is weird creatures everywhere...

Lizann Barretto (12)
Villiers High School, Southall

The Tsunami

It was a dark, stormy night. I was terrified for my life. No one could survive this. Except for me. There was water, floods, a tsunami. It was a total catastrophe. My life was almost over. People were screaming and swimming for survival in the city that had turned into a nightmare. I found a cave, a cave where there was no water. Finally, I was safe, or so I thought. There was someone else there but it wasn't the end, water flooded in...

Jasmin Sandhu (11)
Villiers High School, Southall

Rising Lava

I was in a room full of lava. There was a big, red button in school, I clicked it and entered this room. I realised that the lava was starting to rise, there were blocks so I rushed over and started jumping high. The lava started to get higher and it was coming much quicker than before. I almost fell, but there was a rope above me. I squeezed it, my hands were getting blisters. As I took a step, I saw a hole. I jumped...

Samsuz Zaman (11)
Villiers High School, Southall

The Catastrophic Collapse

It was a catastrophic day. An asteroid had hit the Eiffel Tower and everyone had vanished in the blink of an eye. There was iron everywhere, everything was quiet. The area was dark. I couldn't even tell whether my eyes were open. I kept bumping into broken iron. *Bump!* I did know I was in Paris. I checked my navigation system to show me the way, but it wouldn't tell me. What was going on? What could I do?

Johan Mariyathas (11)
Villiers High School, Southall

The Avalanche

I went to the Antarctic, then it happened. The avalanche. Many people died. Lucky for me, I was one of the survivors. All I had was food, water and a knife. I had no idea what to do. It hit many people, including me. Only ten people survived. My family were there with me but they died. I was in shock and I was thirsty so I drank some water. So many families and friends were all dead. This was the worst day of my life...

Suruthika Baheetharan (12)
Villiers High School, Southall

Lost In Tsunami

I was at home with my family celebrating Christmas when it happened, the tsunami. My name's Rebecca and here's my story.
I finally pulled myself up against a surviving tree, desperate for air. Where was I? *Splash!* A head appeared from the muddy water and pulled himself up against a log.
"Hello," I struggled. He didn't reply. "Hello?" I repeated. "Can you speak?"
He shook his head and forced a weak smile.
A few days passed and I was searching for my family, walking beside the boy. There they were, dead bodies huddled together, bones and flesh...

Jasmine Keyah Sylvan (12)
Woodside High School, Wood Green

The Monster That Destroyed Humanity

Crash! Stomp! The sound of footsteps echoes through the city. The monster tears a path through Tokyo. Its head is hundreds of feet above the ground. Its tail smashes into buildings, sending debris down onto civilians. Cars are crushed like paper under its feet. It's intent on destroying what's left of humanity. Jet fighters send missiles straight into its face, but it doesn't even flinch. Undeterred, it continues its destruction of people's homes. Suddenly, it stops. The spines that run down its back and tail glow green. Then, an explosion of green fire erupts from its mouth, destroying everything nearby...

Luke Chapman (13)
Woodside High School, Wood Green

It's Back: The Whirlpool

The water outside rippled and jolted violently. The seagulls flew gracefully over the pale blue sky as if nothing, let alone a whirlpool, was going on. The wind led her closer to the water's edge, her hair swaying behind her. Buildings crashed helplessly into the hypnotising whirl of water. Everything was falling apart. Her numb fingers stiffened around a pole as her head whirled, like the whirlpool itself, into complete emptiness. *This is it*, she thought as panic struck her. Suddenly, everything felt still. *Very* still. The whirlpool had her and now, it had her for good...

Aziza Hussain Khan (12)
Woodside High School, Wood Green

Elemental Revenge

There have been disasters all over the world. The anger of fire; the jealousy of water; the frustration of earth and the mocking of air. Many lives have been lost. I've seen them all. Tsunamis have invaded the safety of home; fires from the deserts of Texas have ripped through forests, leaving villagers homeless, destroying animal habitats; tornadoes and earthquakes have attacked South America, where I am.

As I get out of the basement and start putting my foot on the harassed grass, a horrendous wind slaps my face, sending me flying into a tree. *Here we go again...*

Ezel Rose Kupeli (11)
Woodside High School, Wood Green

A Tale Of Survival

It has been two days since the earthquake which brought all the continents together but almost totally destroyed them. I have been hunting down survivors in what I think is Phoenix, Arizona. I stride further away from my camp, hoping to find a sign of survival, but no luck so far. Earlier today, I thought I'd found a spiral of smoke luring me to it. My hopes flew up, but my physical state made me rest. I'll check tomorrow.

So I do. It's coming from a nearby cave. I think I've found life. I've found survivors...

Benjamin Kane-Bryant (11)
Woodside High School, Wood Green

Farewell To Earth

Eight years ago, I was watching those horrendous ghastly devils destroying us humans. Our 3482 technology would have saved us if we were prepared. My father made cytoplasma ammunition for our escpasusmian guns. The creatures died, but their kind, even when dead, were deadly. When they died, they turned into black holes! Our fierce warriors were sucked into the darkness as they screamed in agony as they tortured them. Now, only me and three others remain on a small island living on fish. I will avenge them and destroy the creatures forever...

Syaam Hussain (11)
Woodside High School, Wood Green

Rampage

I gazed at the 'cool' kids from the bench. As I wandered to my next lesson, I heard screams. I had no idea where they were coming from. I overheard glass shattering and things falling over. I felt my heartbeat. I rushed outside to see a tornado rampaging through the school playground like a bully shoving a boy! The destruction was massive. Trees fell, rubbish was flying. A girl had tripped over. I immediately helped her up, but she didn't say anything, she just ran. I had no idea what to do. I took out my phone and called Dad...

Patryk Swierad (12)
Woodside High School, Wood Green

Lost In A Tsunami

One summer's day at the beautiful tropical beach in Thailand, we surfed and played beach games. Can you think of a better day? The waves were gigantic. We had an amazing day. I could taste the salty water. I was glad winter was over. Scientists thought that a tsunami might arrive soon, but we were hoping for the best. The sun was orange and yellow, but the crystal clear blue ocean was suddenly overtaken by a tsunami! All of us ran away. The waves took out the cars. Building pieces swirled around our heads. It died quicker than it rose.

Madiha Iman Ahmed (11)
Woodside High School, Wood Green

Sinking Into Darkness

The scorching sky enveloped the clouds as summer bloomed in heat. The Earth was humid. The ground trembled. The world crashed. There was a boy with fear in his eyes. He ran till he trembled like the Earth. Lifeless chunks hit him. It felt like pain was screaming in his ear. Tears escaped from his eyes. Then the only person who loved him disappeared. He saw everything, but it was like he was muted from the world. His life crashed before him. He felt himself sinking into darkness. His life was lost. His mind and sanity became sallow death...

Yasin Dogar (11)
Woodside High School, Wood Green

Reality

Nowhere. An isolated abyss that was soon to end. An enormous factory that was researching natural disasters surrounded me. All of a sudden, the sky turned a radiant burning orange. I knew what was awaiting me - a meteor! My heart was pounding and sweat trickled down my face like a leaky pipe. It all happened so rapidly. The fiery cheetah leapt down on everything below. I tried to restrain myself, however, nothing worked. Everything was over. It had to be a dream! But nothing worked. It wasn't a dream, it was reality...

Charles William Laurence (12)
Woodside High School, Wood Green

YOUNG WRITERS INFORMATION

We hope you have enjoyed reading this book – and that you will continue to in the coming years.

If you're a young writer who enjoys reading and creative writing, or the parent of an enthusiastic poet or story writer, do visit our website **www.youngwriters.co.uk**. Here you will find free competitions, workshops and games, as well as recommended reads, a poetry glossary and our blog.

If you would like to order further copies of this book, or any of our other titles, then please give us a call or order via your online account.

Young Writers
Remus House
Coltsfoot Drive
Peterborough
PE2 9BF
(01733) 890066 / 898110
info@youngwriters.co.uk

Join in the conversation!

 YoungWritersUK    @YoungWritersCW